Catherine F. B. Macready

Leaves from the Olive Mount

Poems

Catherine F. B. Macready

Leaves from the Olive Mount
Poems

ISBN/EAN: 9783337287825

Printed in Europe, USA, Canada, Australia, Japan

Cover: Foto ©Andreas Hilbeck / pixelio.de

More available books at **www.hansebooks.com**

LEAVES FROM THE OLIVE MOUNT.

LEAVES FROM THE OLIVE MOUNT.

Poems

BY

CATHERINE FRANCES B. MACREADY.

———

LONDON:

CHAPMAN AND HALL, 193 PICCADILLY.

1860.

LONDON :

STRANGEWAYS & WALDEN (late G. Barclay). Printers,
28 Castle St. Leicester Sq.

To my Father.

For ever loved, revered,— my heart's first friend,—
Tender as love itself, and true as truth,
I would that men might see thee with my eyes.
Know thee as I have known — then should fame's wreath
(Bound on thy brows of yore) new semblance take,
And show thee halo'd with celestial light!
Yet I, who know thee best, and have enshrined
Thy virtues in my soul, shall feeblest prove
To speak, how dear thy worth!—That which has been
Most noble in thee, never can be known.
Oh, loving lips, long silent in the grave,
Could but the old life warm them for a space,
How would they echo now my poor applause!
And oh, if this adventurous tongue can boast
The transcript of one pure intent, true thought,
Or generous aspiration, unto thee
Alone be praise! All good my life can show
Is of thy teaching, and in offering thee
This lowly tribute of my grateful love,
God knows, I give thee but thine own again!

C. F. M.

In prefixing the title to this little volume, the Author is desirous of disclaiming all pretension to dogmatic assumption, having made use of it simply in allusion to the religious sentiment pervading the following poems.

CONTENTS.

THE PASSION FLOWER .

THE IMAGE OF THE TRUTH .

THE WOODEN CROSS .

CHRIST . . . .

THE ANGEL OF LOVE . .

SPRINGS IN THE DESERT .

THE SIBYL'S PROPHECY .

HEAVEN ? . .

CONSOLATOR . .

ICHABOD . . . . .

THE SHADOW OF THE HAND .

THE POET . . .

DOMENIC . . . .

TO CECILE .

ERRATA.

In Lines " To my Father," v. 14, *for* " tongue " *read* " pen."
Page 14, v. 19, *for* " unlike that" *read* " unlike to that."
Page 20, v. 24, *for* " to beloved" *read* " to be loved."

And bid the drooping Genius of their doom
Doff his dark robes, and to their sight reveal,
White-winged, an angel of benignant mien.
Hearken then, stricken and bereavèd ones!
Ye, that have loved and lost ;—whose lorn hearts ache
With load of mournful memories—to whose eyes
All radiant sights grow dim thro' mist of tears—
Quicken your long-dulled senses, for, behold,
" The wilderness is gladdened. and the birds

B

THE PASSION FLOWER.

PART I

Faint hope is mine with these o'er-plaintive strains
To charm the children of prosperity,
Win tears from eyes as yet unlearned to weep,
Or touch blithe hearts : But, for their sakes, who long
Have lived on life's dark side, fain would I draw
Some drops of balm from sorrow's bitter cup ;
And bid the drooping Genius of their doom
Doff his dark robes, and to their sight reveal,
White-winged, an angel of benignant mien.
Hearken then, stricken and bereavèd ones !
Ye, that have loved and lost :—whose lorn hearts ache
With load of mournful memories—to whose eyes
All radiant sights grow dim thro' mist of tears—
Quicken your long-dulled senses, for, behold,
" The wilderness is gladdened, and the birds

B

Break forth in singing!"   Oh, that I might tune
My voice to their sweet notes; then should my song
Steal, Syren-like, thro' all your inmost souls,
And unaware beguile them of their griefs!

To see before and after—know too much,
And yet too little—suffer in excess,
And taste of joy the veriest ecstasy —
Hope, yearn, and strain for what to others' eyes
Are shadows, fashions of a fevered dream—
Love with a love, before whose fires the light
Of human passion flickers faint and dim,—
Such is the poet's lot;—and such was thine,
Thou child of Light, aspiring Näamah!
Well did thy name become thee, for thou wast,
Ev'n from thy day of birth, "the Beautiful;"
As fair as are the stars on summer night,
As pure as earliest snowdrops,—delicate
As the frail gossamer a breath can stir.
All, earth could boast of rare and fortunate,
From her first dawn of life, was Näamah's.
For tho' long since beyond her memory's reach
Both parents died, her uncle, cold and stern
To all beside, had lavished tenderness
Upon his orphan charge; had been to her
Father and mother, guardian, friend, and guide,
All ties in one: and in due time designed
To bind her yet more closely in his love

By marriage with his heir and favourite son.
Youth, health, and hope, and wealth and high estate,
Rich promise for the future,—all were hers.—
Yet dull and slow of soul are they, who judge
The heart's content by outward shows of bliss.
We have a world within, with sun and stars
And seasons of its own,—where tempests rage
Ofttimes, and all is darkness and dismay,
Whilst o'er our visible life no trouble lies,
But west winds blow, and softening showers descend,
And all is calm, as Eden ere the fall.
Oh, then, be tender with thy blame or scorn,
If haply thou art one to probe the deeps
Of this mysterious being, called our soul,
So full of natural sadness, and so prone
To murmur, whatsoe'er its mortal lot.—
From earliest years, a strange and silent child.
Of mood so mild and still, was Näamah,
She moved like one, upon whose spirit weighs
A sense of wonder, mystery, and awe.
Her large, bright, questioning eyes still seemed to ask
The meaning of the world without her soul,
So much unlike the world she found within.
Aye wrapt in musings and surmisings vague
That found no vent, from day to day she grew
More soul-perplexed and sad, until her mind
Was like to work and wear itself away.
A shadow seemed to lie upon her life,

O'ercasting all she saw, and thought, and felt.
Death seemed too distant — death, that could not fail
To chase the darkness, and beyond disclose
The world of cheerful peace, for which she pined.
So passed her childhood; but her fourteenth year
Had scarcely dawned, when lo! there seemed to break
A sudden radiance on her inward life,
As if some soul-awakening spirit moved
Upon the slumb'ring waters of her mind,
And made its fountains bubble forth afresh.
Her tongue was loosed; — her long so silent lips
Gave forth a gush of such rare eloquence,
That she became a wonder to herself:
So strange it seemed and sweet to find the thoughts,
Long cold and dead, awake to warmth and life,
And fill the air around with melodies.
Now might her lute be heard at eventide,
And voice low murmuring in plaintive rhymes;
Her gliding form be seen at earliest dawn
Low bending o'er her flowers, to watch their cups
Just opening to the sun : but most she loved
To ponder books of sad or grave import,
And picture to her mind in various shapes
Man's mournful destiny, and school her heart
To look on sorrow as our portion here.
Thus deeming life a struggle and a cross
To fight out bravely, patiently to bear,
She ever strove to fix her thoughts beyond

This visible world, and garner up her love
In that all-tender and eternal Heart,
Whence all love flows;—until within her grew
Such certainty of things unseen,—she lived
In presence of some breathing sanctity,
And kept her eyes still steadfast turned towards
The light, that radiates from th' Eternal mind.
All theories of prophet, bard, and sage,
Her ardent mind explored, from every source
Deducing truth, how deep soe'er imbued
And fouled with falsehood, as the miner clears
The costly jewel from its bed of clay;—
Probed to their origin men's various creeds
And superstitions, not with bigot scorn
To shudder at their sad deformities,
But with a lowly reverence for her kind,
And the discerning eye of piety,
That sees thro' every faith, howe'er involved
In darkness and corruptions, traces faint,
Dim shadowings of the One Eternal Truth.
Thus was her life in all enjoyments rich
Of healthful, pure, and elevating kind;
A life so innocent and beautiful,
So guarded from all taint of worldliness,
It seemed, as on some hallowed eminence
Her ark had rested, far above the earth,
Girt round with harmonies and airs of Heav'n.

When Näamah from dreamless slumber woke,
The morn of her betrothment, sunlight streamed
Thro' her green-curtained casement in long streaks
Of emerald on the floor, and odours faint
Stole thro' the open lattice of sweet-brier
And clustering jessamine — and singing birds
Greeted her ears with chorus of blithe notes
And strains mellifluous — till, with heart brim full
Of grateful ecstasy, she clasped her hands,
And cried — " Oh God ! how beautiful is life ! "
Scarce sixteen summers Näamah might count
On this auspicious morn.   She knew some change
Was stealing over life, yet knew not what,
Half pleasant, half perplexing, to a heart
That love as yet had touched not.   She had lived,
As lives a child within its parents' home,
Loving her cousins with a sister's love,
Scarce knowing which, if either, she loved best;
Too happy in the present, much to care
For promise of more happiness to come.
'Twas near the close of spring, the morning wind
Blew soft and cool, when Näamah, attired
In silken robe, like some fair queen of May,
Came forth, as was her wont, to walk at dawn.
She paced the long stone terrace, looking out
Upon the wood-crowned hills with blue mists veiled
(Which slow the sun dispersed), and distant sea,
That sparkled thro' the openings of the trees.

On each side beds of flowers and velvet lawn
Greeted her eyes,—while delicately wreathed
With many-tinted ivy, from the wall
Of the old mansion graceful creepers hung.
Yet spring was almost ended, and she marked,
Half sadly, how so soon the golden chains
Of the laburnum, broken, shed their gems,
With pale syringa petals, on the ground.
" Thus, beauty and decay, and life and death,
On this strange earth are blended!" murmured she ;
When, close at hand, a deep-toned tender voice
Accosted her, and turning, she beheld
Her cousin Wilfred—" All too sad," he said,
" Such thoughts for such a season, my sweet bride !
The fairest morning greets thee, harbinger
Of fairer yet to come !   I would not meet
The future, bright with promise as it seems,
In mood of childish mirth; yet fain would see
The light of sober gladness in thine eyes,
On thy dear lips a smile ; for life with thee
Shall be as bright as this spring morning, love,
And calm as summer evening after showers!"
The colour deepened on the maiden's cheek,
A flush of candid joy : " How sweet," she said.
" Are words of hope from thee ! Methought of late
Some sorrow lay upon thee ; thou wast grown
So still and silent, and thy brow oft knit
In troublous meditation : clouds no more

Obscure thy cheerful soul, and joyfully
I hail thee prophet of good times to be!"
"Ev'n so, my Naamah; yet this bright morn,
Which binds us by so close a tie, foreruns
To-morrow, when reluctantly I bid
Adieu, for many a day, to all I love.
Thou knowest how ardently my father's hopes
Are fixed on me to raise his honoured name
To yet more honour;—how I do aspire,
By toil and constancy, in future days
To lay a wreath of fame at his loved feet.
For this I leave thee, certainly assured
To prove, in truth to him, more true to thee:
And tho' debarred thy presence, in my dreams
I shall behold thy beauty, see thee smile
In fond approval of my studious choice.
Then wonder not, that care and serious thought
Intrude upon my wonted buoyant mood.—
Besides, the thought of her, whom all too ill
I loved when with us, oft revisits me,
Checking too eager mirth; and ere we part,
'Tis ev'n of her, beloved, that I would speak.
Sometimes I smile, but oftener sigh, to think
How in my early boyhood I have looked
With envy on my brother Gabriel's lot,
Who, being weak in health from infancy,
Was kept at home and delicately reared,
While I was forced to fight my way alone

Thro' rough school life.—Night after night I lay
Dejected, picturing to my fancy home,
Its freedom and delights; and thought, how hard
To con my tasks the long hot summer day,
Whilst Gabriel gambolled in the fields at will,
Or sat in shady nook beside the stream.—
I loved my brother, yet I envied him;
And loathed myself the while, and writhed in vain
To free myself (as from a haunting fiend)
From this same griping passion. Yet it lived
And burned within me, and I trembled, lest
By word, or look, or gesture unawares,
I might betray my secret shame. Alas!
I knew not, there were eyes, I could not blind,
Too slow to read their meaning, oftentimes
Fixed on me full of tears, with such a look,
As should have awed the demon from my heart,
And left it free to penitence and love!
Oh, gentle Näamah, hast thou not marked,
When all around was wrought to noisy mirth,
And a low deep-drawn sigh would startle us,
How, laughter checked, all looks would sudden turn
Towards my mother, filled with wonderment?
Those sighs have long found echo in my heart:
God knows, how mournful is their memory!
'Twas the last summer of her life, she sat,
One sunny afternoon, beneath the porch
Where grows the Passion Flower; a pang of grief

Shot thro' my heart at sight of her changed face,
Till then unmarked its wanness : close I knelt
Beside her, bending down my head to hide
The tears that blinded me : she, tenderly
Interpreting my silence, passed her arm
Around my neck, and drew me to her heart.
Oh, hour to be remembered,—after hope,
Ambition's glowing dreams, and all of earth
Most fair and dear, are faded from my thoughts !
In her long wasted hands she folded mine,
And clasped them close, and fixed her eyes, intent
With looks of pleading love, upon my face.
' Thou art thy father's well-beloved,' she said,
' The son, in whom his soul delights :— Thy voice
And presence so resembling his, I seem
To gaze upon the image of his youth
Renewed in thee ; ah, as thou hast encroached
Upon thy feebler brother's share of love,
And seest him poor, wherein thou most art rich,
Thyself fill up the void, and be to him
In tenderness as brother, parent, guide,
Companion, all in one : curb his wild thoughts,
Strange phantasies, and gently win his mind
To sober exercise and wise pursuits,
That he may grow in thy dear father's love,
Who deems him vain and indolently bent;
(Too harshly judging him !) therefore do thou,
For my poor memory's sake, at all times seek

To shield thy brother from cold looks, and scorn,
And stern rebuke ;—for grief in one so frail
Would wear away the slender threads of life,
And lay him early at his mother's side.'
Her looks are graven on my heart ; her tones,
Like voices of the unseen world, vibrate
Upon my inward sense unceasingly!
For this, in absence I would fain bequeath,
To *thee* this sacred trust, loved Näamah,
Beseeching thee (as thou wast ever prone
To kindly offices) that thou wilt be
As guardian saint to my poor Gabriel,
And by the fair example of thy life
Attract him upwards to the paths of truth,
Such feet as his and thine were formed to tread !"
With downcast eyes, as one abashed by sense
Of her own failings, and in tremulous tone,
The willing Näamah her promise gave.
And now they neared the house, and paused beneath
The porch, where wreathes the Passion Flower,—
        "Wear this
Among thy braids of auburn hair, beloved,"
Said Wilfred, reaching out his hand to cull
The fairest blossom ; when an eager voice
Cried, close behind them, " Wilfred, hold thine hand !
Pluck not, touch not the baleful Passion Flower !
'Twas planted by an enemy, and reared
By th' evil genius of our house : wrong not

Thy bride with such a gift on such a morn!"
"Away with thy wild fancies, Gabriel!"
Returned the elder brother, " in my heart
I hold it dear, this sacred Passion Flower!
My mother taught me as a child to trace
Within its cup the cross and crown of thorn,
Which one day must be borne by all who live.
Heed him not, Näamah; ev'n as these leaves
Unfold their glories 'neath the mid-day sun,
So shall thy life, like this propitious morn,
Be ripened into splendour at its noon."

The sounds of festival had died away,
The farewells spoken : Wilfred pensive stood,
In the grey dawn, beside his mother's grave.
Behind him rose the time-stained sombrous pile,
Which late had rung to song and merriment,
Now silent as a tomb.   Enchantment sure,
The scene of yesternight; the shining halls,
Fair forms, that moved in gem-embroidered vest
To sound of music, as their voices sweet,
Gay as their hopes—it seemed, a magic wand
Had wafted all that fairy world away,
While memory mocked the victim of the spell,
Now waked to sigh o'er life's illusive dreams!
Low bending, Wilfred plucked with reverent hand
A glowing hearts-ease from his mother's grave,
And pressed it to his lips.   " Oh, if thou still

Lovest me, mother! if my feeble prayers
Yet reach thee where thou art, give me, I pray,
Thy blessing ere I go! Too well thou know'st,
With all my good intent, how frail I am,
And prone to err.—How still the world doth lie!
Methinks I feel thy breath upon my cheek,
Hear thy low sigh responsive on the air!
Farewell, beloved spot! thou home, where hope
And memory dwell! within thy shelt'ring walls
She sleeps, my heart's dear all—my love—my bride,—
My wife that shall be! Sleep—sleep on—sweet soul!
God give thee rest—such rest, as angels know,
Who love and sin not! I am sad at heart,
To think how long the days and nights will be,
Ere I shall see thy face!" Thus Wilfred spoke,
Cast one fond ling'ring look on all around,
And turned upon his way reluctantly.
But hope was young within him, and his feet
Still pressed the soil of Eden.—'Tis most true,
Like our first parents in the spring of life,
(Girt in with flowers and breathing perfumed air,)
We deem ourselves in some fair Paradise,
Till sin or sorrow with a sword of flame
Dispels the flatt'ring dream, and drives us forth
To meet the rude realities without,
And toil and weep from morn till evening's close,
When feeble rays of hope beyond this earth
Fall from the silent and mysterious stars.

Into the world went Wilfred ; from his home —
His quiet happy home — that purer world,
Where he could hear God's voice among the trees,
Or in the murmuring rivulet, and read
His lessons in all good and lovely things,
Into that other world, by evil made
A blot in God's creation ; which throughout
Was good in the beginning, until man
With tainted breath marred all he breathed upon !
Oh, man ! too vain and stubborn to obey
The wholesome laws of nature, which alone
Decree thee health, and peace, and happiness,
See what a web thou'st woven round thyself
Of shadows and deceptions ! thro' what maze
Of follies, and hypocrisies, and lies,
Thou hast doomed thy better self with fruitless toil
To seek that truth, which, sunlike, shed its light
So bountiful upon thee at thy birth !
Ah, how unlike that, which thou call'st life,
The life, which God ordained thee ! hadst thou been
But the meek child, that follows trustingly
Its father's voice, how gently might thy days
Have glided by from childhood to old age !
How tenderly His hand, that placed thee here
(When thine appointed mission was fulfilled)
Had drawn thee to himself, thy being's source !
But thou wouldst not ; and lo ! thine history
Is writ in blood and tears ! and the same voice,

That on the doomèd city woe denounced
Of old time, still is heard condemning thee,
Thou world at enmity with Truth and God!
Ye rulers! that so high above your kind
Sit royally enthroned, and on the poor
" Bind heavy burdens grievous to be borne,"
Have ye not ears to hear it ? Sounds it not
Above the treacherous praises of mean men,
Who curse you in their hearts, the while they praise ?
Ye priests, that in your arrogance block up
The entrance to God's kingdom! ye blind guides,
That miss yourselves " the straight and narrow way,"
And suffer none to find it,—steals it not
Athwart the stormy music of the choir,
Vain repetitions, chant monotonous
Of babbling worshippers, even in your souls
Saying, " Your new moons and your solemn feasts
I utterly abhor ; nor dwell I here
In temple made with hands, but in that heart,
That worships me in spirit and in truth ?"
Oh, Caiaphas' disciples, and not Christ's,
That in His name (who plied a lowly trade
Long years in Nazareth, and lived on earth
A wand'rer, minist'ring to despisèd wants
In haunts obscure, amid forsaken souls)—
Now dwell in palaces and make long prayers,
Exhorting to obedience, and to faith
In your misrule, the poor beguilèd crowd,

That gape in ignorant wonder at your feet!
When ye shall lay aside your worldly pomps,
Forsake the throne, whereon, in God's own house,
Your presence gives the lie to all ye teach
Of Christian meekness,—when ye shall bring down
Your pampered wills, and with your own hands work
The meanest offices of charity,
Call Christ your master then, and only then!
Alas! all flesh has erred and gone astray!
Men's doctrine and opinions rule mankind,
And evil, good, and good is evil called;
And he, who would not taint his purer soul
In the foul atmosphere of worldly men,
Must stand aloof in God's own armour dight,
And work in lonely strength his upward way.
Such brave intent had Wilfred—steadfastly
Amid the muddy waters of the world
To make himself a channel clean and pure,
And steer his course within it : so to live
Among men, but not of them, ardently
Within his Master's vineyard labouring
Thro' the mid heat and burden of the day.
At length well-earned success his efforts crowned:
Applause beyond expectance greeted him.
In science, art, and all fair enterprise
He won the palm; while young men chafed, and old
Wearied not praising him; and mothers sighed,
And eyed him enviously, with wistful hope,

That God might give them such a son as he!
The wise and good, (choice spirits of the earth,)
Proclaimed him of their brotherhood, and paid
Delighted homage to a youth, so rich
In all the excellence of ripened years.
Fain had they sometime shared his leisure hours:
But Wilfred, conscious of his frailty, feared
To face the flatt'ring aspect of his fame,
Lest, dazzled unawares, his soul should stoop
From lofty heights of modesty to pride.
So, as in sanctuary enshrined, he lived—
Fanning ambition to a holy flame: —
The gentle presence of his living love,
And his dead mother's spirit haunting him,
Still prompting high endeavour—pointing out
To peaceful home and pleasures innocent,
His guerdon in the future: thus fulfilled
The utmost promise of his sanguine youth,
The years of his probation wore away.

Meanwhile a free blithe life had Gabriel led
In Näamah's companionship: at will
Following his fancies, ofttimes wand'ring lone
O'er heath and moor from morn till fall of eve;
Among the rocks by moonlight, lulled his soul
To the low music of the rippling sea.
A joyous child of nature: one, who dwelt
Too much apart from human sympathy

c

In his own world : his father oft from home,
His priestly tutor loving more to wield
The sword of controversy, than to guide
His wayward charge up learning's steep ascent ;
None seemed to care which way he wander'd, how
His hours were spent, poor youth, save Näamah,
Whom Wilfred's parting tenderness had bound
In promise to befriend him.   Guilelessly
She strove that promise to fulfil, nor deemed
(As stronger natures still the weaker sway)
The change, she sought to work in Gabriel's soul,
Wrought in her own, attuning it to his
In perfect harmony.   Day after day,
What keen delight was theirs, when side by side
On greensward bank reclined, they conned the page
Of old romance,—rare tales of chivalry,
And fairy lore — until the scene around
Seemed all alive with fancied forms of knights,
And high-born dames in gorgeous quaint attire ;
While white plumes danced, and jewelled corslets
        gleamed
Between the trees, and every shrub and flower
To them was consecrate, the favoured haunt
Of elf and fay,—each moss-grown well and spring
And gurgling brook the choice resort of nymph,
Or soulless water-sprite !   How pleasing sad,
Moved by the bard's enchanting art, to weep
With gentle Tancred his Clorinda's fate,

Or with forlorn Erminia wand'ring lone,
The prey of hopeless love! To blend their sighs
O'er Petrarch's plaintive strains in praise of her,
The gold-haired Laura, cold embodiment
Of the divine idea in his mind!
Ofttimes at evening, when the wind's sweet breath
Had cooled the air, in a small pleasure-boat
They drifted out upon the tranquil sea,
And sat, in silence musing, till the shades
Of twilight gathered round the tall grey cliffs,
And dimmed the distant shore: such calm supreme
Their souls pervaded,—sense of solemn awe,
As though some spirit mighty and benign
Brooded upon the deep: or He, who trod
Erect the stormy waves of Galilee,
Had left His viewless track upon the sea,
And lulled its heavings in profound repose.
Such hours of bliss, serene, unspeakable,
Snatched from the dull routine of daily life,
Brief foretaste seemed of that sublimer state,
Towards which our yearnings tend! How beautiful
Was Gabriel's face in moments such as these!
But most, when in the chapel, soul-enwrapt,
With wondrous skill he waked the organ-tones,
While mellowed light thro' painted windows streamed
Upon his rare pale features, luminous
With inspiration's glow, a transient gleam
Of such seraphic radiance, as might bless

The eyes of Raphael in ecstatic trance,
Or Milton in his dreams of Paradise!
Why thrills thy bosom, Näamah, and tears
Fill thy clear eyes?   Ah, me! some lips there are
With power to frame our unformed fancies, give
Our vague emotions utterance : some eyes,
Interpreting and answering with a look
Of mutual exaltation and despair
Our soul's aspirant questionings, and moods
Of deep despondency! by such great gift
Are poets, like their father-prophets, made
" Revealers of the thoughts of many hearts."
Yet sunshine will not always last : and oft,
When Gabriel chanced to meet his father's gaze
Fixed on him full of scorn and stern reproof,
His fragile frame would droop, his cheek grow wan,
Sunken and haggard, lustreless his eye ;
His blithe soul seemed to shrink and wither up
As it were blighted, and the springs of joy
All dried within him.   Silent, motionless,
Dejected, he would sit ; or, if he spoke,
His dirge-like tones would wring her to the heart.
" Leave me, sweet Näamah," he oft would say,
" I was not made like Wilfred to beloved,
The heir of fame and honours ; on my birth
No star of promise shone.   I feel my life
Is strung on such a frail and feeble thread,
A breath would part it : wherefore should I live ?

To live unloved is but to fill the place
Of worthier spirits, and to cumber earth.
Methinks we never wholly love our friends,
Until they die. Ah, then we cease to think,
That e'er they vexed or grieved us; nothing lives
But memory of their tenderness and truth
And patience towards us. Would that I were dead!
Then would my father's heart in pity melt!
Then haply he would love me, and the thought,
That, tho' unworthy, I was still his son,
Would draw a blessing down upon my grave.
Dost weep? Weep not, kind sister! never bend
Thy fair head to the earth for my poor sake.
I thought not to beguile thee of a sigh,
And for thy precious tears, such eyes as thine
Were never made to weep, save tears of joy!"

Bodes it not ill, beneath the Passion Flower
To sit in silence, while the village bells
Make merry music for the heir's return?
Have the years sped too swiftly, or is he,
Once held so dear, no longer welcome home?
Where are the voices eloquent with love,
And sparkling looks, that should have greeted him,—
Well-earned reward of one so brave and true?
Rings not the question thro' thy shudd'ring soul,
Unhappy Näamah! while up thy cheeks
And o'er thy bended brow the burning blush

Quick mantles?   Ah, not years, not a long life
Of human bliss, had recompensed the pangs
Of that distressful hour!   With trembling frame
Heart-sick the maiden sat; till Gabriel,
All anguish-stricken, like to one that starts
From some wild dream, in passionate accents cried,
" Have I not loved him? Answer, Näamah!
Thou know'st how gladly, but for his dear sake,
I had lain quiet in my mother's grave!
What was this vacant, loveless world to me,
Save when his presence, like a spot of green,
Gladdened life's desert? now, as if my soul
Were stained with some foul sin, I shrink and writhe
At thought of meeting him! Oh, pity me!
My heart will burst, my brain seems all on fire!
God knows, too late *I love thee*, and too well!"
Pale, statue-like, sat Näamah :—the past
Before her fancy vividly arose
With glare reproachful! all its happy days
(Of aspect late so fair and innocent)
Seemed haunted by the ghost of broken vows,
Till then unheeded quite. No word she spoke,
But pressed her damp cold hands upon her brow
To quell the agony, that burned within.
" Look not so strangely; speak, I pray thee, speak,
Beloved Näamah!—I cannot bear
To see thee thus. Fear not; this passion dire,
Which racks my soul, shall never hurt thy peace!

No! by my faith in thy sweet self, thy truth,
Thy saintly purity, this hour I swear,
I will fly from thee, hide my stricken life,
Where never sight or thought of me shall give
Thy heart one pang. Oh, love! oh, misery!
Know'st thou not, I would die to save thee pain!"

"Then leave me not!" said Näamah, her voice
Half-choked with sobs. "Thou know'st not what thou
    say'st.
If it be guilt to love thee, then am I
Past pardon guilty,—wretched beyond cure!
When with thy brother first I plighted troth,
Alas, I knew not what it was to love!
And tho' my sin be great, forsake me not!—
How can I bear the weight of it alone?
Far better, happier, side by side to lie
On death's cold bosom, than to live apart,
Now that my soul is grafted upon thine.
To see thee, hear thee, speak to thee no more,
Would be no more to hear, to speak, to live!"

The lark was flutt'ring up the evening sky,
Startling the silent air from time to time
With its delicious music; farewell rays
Of dying sunlight pierced the tall tree-tops,
And tinged the upland slopes, while dewy mists
Crept o'er the vale beneath. Past wood and stream,

By the green hill-side, filled with happy thoughts,
Slow wended Wilfred, pausing oft, to greet
After long absence each familiar scene,
To love and hope and memory consecrate.
His pace he quickened as the massive front
Of the old mansion cheered his longing sight.
Now thro' the dark'ning avenue,— across
The lawn,— by beds of closing flowers—
He hurried, breathless with expectancy;
Sprung on the terrace, gained the open door,
And the next moment in his father's arms
Close locked, with blessings tremulous, could feel
The old man's tears and kisses on his face.

The lamps are lighted in the old oak hall,
With costly cheer the table spread, festooned
The lofty walls with flowers and garlands green,
To grace the wanderer's return. With eyes
Brim-full of love his father gazed on him,—
" Why grow thy lips so white ? what ails my son ?
Behold, thy bride, thy brother, welcome thee !
Speak to him, daughter ! Gabriel, give him joy
For all the honour he has won our house,
Himself its chiefest praise and ornament!"
None moved; none spoke; a gloom mysterious seemed
To gather thro' the chamber; trouble sat
On each young brow. With wonder Wilfred marked
The fever-spot that glowed on Gabriel's cheek,

His eye's unnatural restless brilliancy,
His dry-hot hands and vague perturbèd look,
While Naamah all pale, with circlets dark,
The trace of passionate tears, around her eyes,
Perplexed him with a thousand nameless fears.
He cast on each, by turns, imploring looks,
Well-nigh bewildered : not a word, a smile,
In answer to his fond appeal! ah, me!
What mute despair was his, when, unawares,
A glance of mutual pity and dismay
Exchanged between the lovers, startled him
To recognition of the fatal truth!
How ghastly grew his cheek! his quiv'ring lip!
Red gleams of angry fire flashed from his eye!
A chilling tremor ran thro' all his frame,
His limbs waxed icy cold — the hall, the lights,
All forms familiar swam before his eyes —
His reason for a moment stunned by stroke
Of such unlooked-for, overwhelming doom!
He sprang upon his feet with look distraught,
And staggered out into the cool night air.

Ah, Wilfred! whither wilt thou go — dispelled
Thy summer dream of love ? — waked with rude start
To face the keen blasts of this wintry world,
And find the flowers all gone ?   Away! away!
How far he heeds not: blackest darkness seems
To press upon his sight,—the atmosphere

Is clogged, and stifles him; he gasps for breath;
Air, air, and light! he leapt the outer wall,
Rushed down the steep with headlong speed, across
The meadows and the stony flats, climbed up
The perilous cliffs whose crags o'erhang the sea,
Till, faint and panting with the toil, he lay
On the green turf that crowned the precipice;
Discordant passions preyed upon his soul,
Love, envy, agony of blighted hopes.
Hatred and wrath (like goading fiends) possessed
His gentle nature, loath to entertain
Such hellish visitants.   Worn out at last
A stupor fell upon him, giving place
After a while to a deep sleep, and dream
Of softening influence: he thought, he lay
Within the well-known chamber, where he slept
In happy boyhood: close beside the bed
His mother, bending down, stood watching him;
Her eyes were fixed on his, so large and blue,
So like his brother Gabriel's! her hair
In long pale ringlets touched the coverlid.
He longed to call her "mother," but his tongue
Refused its utterance; lovingly he sought
To clasp her, but his arms were stiff and weak,
And in the fruitless effort he awoke.

"Oh thou of days remembered! dost thou come
With thy sweet looks to chide, or comfort me?"

The moon is risen: the earth beneath its beams
Grows beautiful as fairy land! the sea
Among the rocks makes murmur musical.
Thou grand consoler, Nature! speak to him!
Teach him, how slight a thing is human life,
With all its loves and anguish, in the scale
Of Being infinite! how shrink its cares,
Its vain concernments, empty promises,
In presence of the solemn night, the sea,
That, imaging eternity, rolls on,
(From earliest dawn of immemorial time,
When first God's Spirit moved upon its face,)
While generations of mankind decay.

THE PASSION FLOWER.

PART II.

How sorrowful is life! ah, how unlike
Its morning expectation! long ere noon
The skies are clouded, and the heavy rain
Beats down the flowers to perish in their bloom!
Men say, it is God's curse, that, like a blight,
Has fallen upon the earth, and turned to gall
All it may bear of sweetness;—'tis God's curse,
That disappoints life's glorious promises,
And makes our natural instincts, even our hope
And love, a source of shame and agony!
Thus they arraign His gentle providence
For all the nameless ills themselves have wrought,
And mock Him with lip-service, saying "God"
(Which meaneth good), "Lift up thy vengeful hand,
Which presseth sore and weighs us down to hell."
As if 'twere possible for good to curse,
Or love to hate, or mercy to revenge,

Or God, who is Himself the Soul of Good,
And Love, and Mercy, to do aught but bless!
His very chastisements are blessings, sent
In token of His presence! everywhere
Is heav'n, where He is! there alone is hell,
Where not a murmur of His voice is heard,
A vestige of His glory seen, nor felt
An emanation of His peace. Behold,
How beautiful are all things He has made!
How marvellously ordered! from the vast,
In measureless expanse beyond our ken,
Ev'n to the insect atom, that eludes
Our straining vision! Life itself was joy,
As God ordained it, to all things that live ;
To the wild beast, that in its freedom ranged
Gigantic forests, tracts immensurate
Of marsh and wilderness ; th' innocent birds,
Nature's interpreters, that in their songs
Convey her silent gratitude to heaven,
And the rare insect tribes that buzz around,
Delighted in the summer's balmy air, —
All, all were happy, until murderous man
Their rights invaded, and with tyrant hand
Brought death and discord on the peaceful earth.
From men's vile passions springs the only curse
That desolates the world, and dooms his soul
To self-created hell; they only come
Between him and the blessing breathed by God

On all His works;—they form the dark abyss,
That mortal from immortal life divides,
Which else were one ; death but the bright ascent,
The Patriarch's ladder leading to the skies!
What more, O man, could parent do for child,
Than God has done for thee, His graceless son ?
He made thee strong of limb, and beautiful
In form and aspect, pure in heart and mind,
And placed thee in a paradise of peace
And healthful joys; and when thou didst break loose
From His just laws, and on thy wretched race
Entailed unnumbered woes and agonies,
He sent His saving Spirit in the guise
Of Mary's gentle child, His Holy One
In human garb with heavenly grace endued,
To teach thee how, ev'n yet, thou might'st restore
His image in thyself, and make the earth
Once more the Eden of its earlier years.
Ah me! how changed were this, our sad estate,
If, (Christ our Master,) we as brethren dwelt!
How sorrow, separation, pain, and death
Would lose their bitterness, could we but know,
That, members of one suffering family,
Each for the other felt, and wept, and prayed!
How soon the songs of mourning would be hushed,
And strife would cease, and strains of peace and love,
" The turtle's voice," be heard in every land!
But for poor mortals, prodigals, that long

Have left their Father's mansion, hope is vain
Of such blest change : Thy chosen servants, Lord !
Thy prophets they have scourged and mocked, and
      stoned,
And for Thy last, the Mighty One, who spake
As ne'er man spake, has He not been to them
" But as a very lovely song of one,
That hath a pleasant voice, and playeth well
Upon an instrument ? for with their ears
They hear his words,—hear, but they heed them not !

All night the wakeful Naamah had paced
Her chamber, listening eager for the sound
Of Wilfred's footsteps in the court beneath,
Hoping, yet dreading his return.   Her heart
Was filled with troublous thoughts and vague alarm;
For him—herself—but most for Gabriel.
" Now will his brother's love, so dearly prized,
Be turned to gall and jealous enmity !
And I have robbed him of his only friend !
Even I—ill-fated one ! whose love does seem
Ever to draw most misery on the head,
It most would bless !—Sure, if unwittingly
I err against that good, which rules my life
(To whom the first place in my heart is due),
'Tis even in the ecstasy of love
I feel for him—for Gabriel !—Oh, Thou,
That hast made him so beautiful and wise,

And worthy to be loved, be pitiful,
If that my weak ill-guided heart at times
Break loose from thy calm influence, and burn
With fires of love too fierce and turbulent!
What would I — would I not endure for him?
Even the loss of that which fills my life,
His love, his presence! ay, and more than these,
(Last, dearest solace!) my own love for him!"
Wearied with watching, Näamah at length
Unbarred her casement, leaning out to cool
Her burning forehead in the fresh night air.
" Oh life! what hast thou to outweigh in bliss
The pain of hours like these?   Ye gentle stars,
That make the night far lovelier than day,
How thro' the darkness, that hems in my soul,
Your rays have stol'n with reassuring light!
I feel the stillness (like God's presence) pass
Into my spirit!   Oh, thou most fair night,
The very soul of him I love doth seem
Expressed in thee! so dreamy, bright, and calm,
Of influence easier felt than understood,
Unutterably lovely and benign!"
But soon the scene was changed—clouds coursed the
        sky —
The shadows darkened, and the stars went out.
The anxious mood returned on Näamah,
And when at length the dawn broke dismal grey,
And still no Wilfred came, she wrung her hands;

"His father's heart will break for love of him!"
How will she meet the old man's mournful looks,
Herself the source of so much misery?
With stealthy tread, as fearing to arouse
The slumb'ring household, she her chamber left,
Stole down the stairs, and pausing at the door
Of Gabriel's study, thought she heard a sob.
She listened,—all was silent;—warily
The latch she lifted, and beheld within
Her lover at his desk with folded arms,
And head bowed down despondently:—all damp
And lustreless his light gold curls, the veins
High swoll'n upon his pale and feverish hands,
His breathing quick and faint.   To Näamah
The very embodiment of grief he seem'd—
Her heart yearned towards him with compassionate love.
She drew near noiselessly, and laid her hand,
All trembling, tenderly upon his arm :
Aroused by her soft touch he started up,
His haggard eyelids steeped with recent tears,
His fair cheek pale and sunken,—gazed on her
(As he would speak and could not) with a look
Heart-rending of remorse, and love, and pain,
And placed an open letter in her hand.
The sight of Wilfred's well-known characters
Awoke fresh sorrow in her o'er-wrought mind.
Her head drooped down, as she were fain to hide
From him, whose love she had so dearly bought,

D

The pangs, that love now cost her:—large warm dr‹
Fell from her eyes, and blistered all the page,
While thus with fearful breathless haste she read.

" I cannot write to Näamah.   Do thou
Bid her farewell for me, and take this ring,
The token of her faith once pledged to mine,
Henceforth thine own.   Oh, if the sight of it
Give thee but half the joy it gave to me,
I somewhat am repaid for my great loss
In thy yet greater gain.—Some tears, alas!
The page have blotted—human eyes must weep!
Yet never heed them, Gabriel.   For me,
I do believe in God, not Destiny—
Nor blame, nor question aught, nor owe thee grudge
For that which He has given, not thou usurped.
As yet I cannot meet thee as I would—
I've written to our father, praying him
To smile upon thy love, and prosper it.
And ev'n so soon as I can school my heart
To think of Näamah as of thy wife,
I will return to the belovèd hearth,
And greet her as my sister.   So, farewell!"

She clasped the letter to her throbbing breast:
Enwrapt she stood, as if the words had wrought
A change throughout her soul, and touched therein
A latent spring of thought serene and brave.

"So good! so grand! so merciful!" she said;
"He is not one of us, but, as a saint
Enshrined in his own sanctity, looks down,
Forbearing and compassionate on those,
Whose frail and feeble powers must ever fail
To reach the heights of such rare nobleness!
Have we not wept enough, my Gabriel?
And who are we, that we should weep for him?
So far above our pity, placed aloft
Our load-star, heav'nward still to beacon us?
Aye, rather daily let us seek to prove
Ourselves more worthy in his sight, and show,
Such high example was not set in vain!"

Low at her uncle's feet bent Näamah,
With tearful eyes and pleading hands upraised,
In hope to soothe the old man's wrathful mood.
But prayers nor tears availed: with gestures fierce
He spurned her from him,—"Hence, inconstant girl!
Falsest of thy false sex!—where are thine eyes,
Thy soul, thy senses? dost thou dream, or rave,
Thus to cast off the noblest gentleman,
The kindest, bravest, for a wayward boy,
A thing of whims and fancies, weak and vain,
And fickle as thyself?   It cannot be
But that thou wilt repent!—thy plighted vows,
Duty and honour, urge thee to keep faith
With my dear Wilfred.   Näamah, be wise!

Ev'n now, wilt thou but yield thy stubborn will,
Forsake the foolish youth that has beguiled
Thy better sense (and is as far outshone
By Wilfred, as the stars are by the sun),
I will forgive, forget, and take thee back,
Child, daughter, darling of my heart, once more."
—In broken accents answered Näamah:
" Alas! that I should live to give thee pain,
That hast been father, mother, all in all,
Tender beyond all thought and good to me!
I would I might obey thee! but my love
Will not be servant to my will.   In vain
I have prayed day and night, that God would warm
My heart towards Wilfred: I have sorely striven
Against this most unhappy love I bear
To him, thou lovest not! oh, he had need,
That one at least on this unpitying earth
Should call him 'friend!' and, as I do believe
My love for him is holy, God-inspired,
So blush I not to own it.   Heav'n and earth
May know that I love Gabriel, as I love
All that is innocent, and fair, and wise!
Oh, just to all but him! thou dost him wrong,
Most bitter wrong!   Couldst thou but read his soul
As I have read it, thou wouldst find therein
Such store of wisdom, nobleness, and truth,
Thou wouldst be fain to worship him like me!"
—Now burned the old man's ire beyond control:

" Begone ! ungrateful and rebellious girl !
False to thyself, to Wilfred, and to me !
The fate I had hoped for thee was far too high
For thy mean spirit. Go : and if thou canst,
Console thee for the friend, whom thou hast lost,
In him, whom thou hast chos'n ! For Gabriel,
His mother's wealth is his :—let him begone,
And take thee with him, faithless as thou art !"

There was no bridal feast, nor gaudy show,
Nor glitt'ring troop of guests, to grace the day
Of Gabriel's marriage with his Näamah.
Yet lovelier, tenderer pair ne'er plighted troth
Before God's altar. She, in pure white robe,
With myrtle-leaves and lilies in her hair,—
Her eyes,—thro' tears of blended joy and grief,
That sweet content expressed,—were fixed on him,
Her life's protecting angel, Gabriel !
His presence filled her soul, nor needed she
A crowd of gaping witnesses to mark
How dear she loved him : 'twas enough, that heav'n
And earth smiled on them, that the morning sun
Shone halo-like upon her lover's brow,
And tinged the walls and marble floor with gold :
And, as they passed out from the chapel door,
The flowers upon their pathway seemed to bend
Their heads in greeting, and the lightsome song
Of birds rung all around them, omens sure

Of peace and blessing on their married life.
" Farewell, beloved home ! familiar haunts,
To childhood's sports and youth's romantic hours
So long devote !—full loath we are to leave
Thy leafy groves and bowers !—and wheresoe'er
Our feet may wander o'er this desolate earth,
In dreams and waking thoughts, with grateful love,
Thine exiled children will remember thee !"

Hard by the Abbey Church in ancient days
Rose the grey walls of Morton Priory ;
Its very name now grown an old wife's tale,
For vestige none remains to mark the spot,
Where once the venerable building stood.
Still, are you one, whose fancy loves to pore
O'er times long past, and tales of antique date,—
There is the orchard, and the clear still pool,
Scarce changed methinks since the dark-hooded friars
Glided beneath the trees, or paused at noon
To trace the shadows of their rosaries
Reflected in the still and liquid pool.
Now, hidden in the orchard, ivy-grown,
And twined with clematis, a cottage stands,
A pleasant rural dwelling-place, fit haunt
For votary of solitude and peace.
There might you live, and dream your days away,
All undisturbed, save by the songs of birds,
Or by the tolling of the Abbey-bell

At morn or fall of eve : a sweeter spot,
Or more serene, methinks you could not find!
To this obscure retreat, far, far away
From kindred, home, and friends, came Gabriel
With his fair bride ; and, oh! on this sad earth
Was never human pair so blest as they!
Shut out from the world's tumult, safe from care,
Discord, and strife, their glad days glided on :
Each in the other finding all content,
They needed none beside their bliss to share.
Said Gabriel, " Our life has long been blest
With special joys! Yet this does overpass
All thought or hope my heart had nursed, and makes
The earth too much, as if it ne'er had lost
Its primal benediction! favoured thus,
Let us not deem this sunny season given
But to enjoy: the longest life is short,
And each hour precious! if we sow not now
Good seed, what harvest shall we reap but shame,
When God shall judge our labours at the last?"
With such sincere intent, night after night,
Until the lamp burnt low, did Gabriel hold
High converse with the spirits of the past,
Pore o'er the classic page, until his eyes
Waxed dim with too much toil, and the red spot
Burned on his cheek ; and then would Näamah
Chide him by turns, and pray him rest awhile,
Lest his too ardent spirit should outwear

The feeble frame that held it. " Never plead
With those distressful looks and those moist eyes
Against the promptings of my holier hours !"
—Thus would he answer: "Trust me, love, high thoughts
(Which are but Virtue's semblance, not herself)
Suffice not without fruit of holy deeds.
Thus poets cheat themselves ; too oft content
With fair resolves and lofty utt'rances,
Discerning wisdom, yet themselves unwise,
As 'twere enough to feel and know the right,
Teach it to others, worship it in words,
Do all, but practise it.   We have great need
To be for ever pondering our estate,
That are of yesterday, and nothing know.
For we may climb the highest heaven of thought,
The boundless fields of speculation range,
Drink living waters at Truth's fountain-head,
And yet fall headlong from our proud ascent,
To end in darkness even as we began !
True faith is of the heart ; a spark of fire,
Lit by that central sun, that animates
And soul-inspires the universe ! a spark
Feeble at first, and kindled to a flame,
Not by ecstatic fancies, heavenward bursts
Of aspiration — no : nor yet by flights
Of lofty intellect, but godly lives,
And child-like following of His law, who taught
' Obey, and by obedience rise to faith !'

Long, silent, ponder'd Naamah his words,
And laid them up like jewels in her mind—
Priceless—wherewith to pave her heavenward way.
She grew more earnest ever; cumbered not
Like Martha, with much serving, yet each day
She failed not in her ministry of love
To all around her. Household cares, that sit
So comely upon woman, homeliest acts
Of peace and kindness, trivial charities,
Assumed in her the rank of loftier deeds,
Graced and exalted by the high intent
With which she wrought them. She had chos'n indeed
The "better part" with Mary: every thought,
And word, and action of her simple life
Was, as it were, a prayer, a song of praise,
A lively sacrifice of love to Heaven.
It might be said of her, that all day long
She sat "in spirit" at the feet of Christ,
Pond'ring His teachings and obeying them.
She tended with untiring tenderness
The sick and poor, and taught the village school,
And gathered round her upon holidays
A group of merry children in the fields,
And showed them games, and sung them pleasant songs,
And simple hymns; ofttimes would tales repeat
Of Christ among the flowers of Palestine,
And how He loved all gentle things, and blessed
The little children clustered at His knee.

Nor feared she in abodes of guilt and shame
To plant her delicate feet, and 'mong the lost
(Long sunk in infamy) to speak of hope,
And peace, and restoration to God's love:
Herself the soul of purity, whose breath
(As 'twere an angel's) cleared the tainted air,
Diffusing sense of sanctity around.
She deemed it not reproach to stand alone,
As Christ stood, with the wretched and the vile,
And plead His promises of better life.
Nor scorn, nor chaste reproof upon her lip,
But beaming thro' the tears in her mild eyes
Compassion lowly, tender, womanly,
Oft would she take within her own the hand
Of some poor erring sister, bowed to earth
With sense of wrong and hopeless misery:
Oft would she kneel beside her, flushed with zeal
Affectionate, and in heart-soothing tones
(All strange to such forlorn one) bid her trust
In Him, who "wrote upon the ground,"—whose words
(Amid the cruel and bloodthirsty throng,
Fiends panting for their prey) struck awe and shame
Into each coward self-accusing heart,—
" Let him that has not sinned, first cast a stone!"
"Not one, but all have erred! in secret some —
And some in open day—and nought of guilt,
Whether of thought or deed, is hid from God,
Who reads the heart.   Therefore will thou and I,

Each for the other, pray, each needing aid
And pity and forgiveness at His hand,
Who having made us, knows how frail we are."
By such devout and meek endeavour, oft
Had she raised up a hapless fallen one
From most degraded depths of wretchedness,
Into the healthful blessèd atmosphere
Of godly life. Nor wonder 'twas, that such,
Scorned outcasts—scarce discerning good from ill—
For the first time beholding Virtue's self
So fair in mortal lineaments expressed,
Should grow enamoured of its loveliness,
And strive with trembling hearts to frame their lives
In faint and dim similitude with hers.
Thus Näamah her unobtrusive works
Of piety pursued; thus, rich in grace
Of mind and mien, she grew from year to year,
Laying up store of recollections bright,
Sure comforters against the evil days.

Where turn our thoughts in all distress and pain,
When mortal love deceives us? when the leaves,
Which hope puts forth so green and fresh in spring,
Lie in dead heaps upon our path, long ere
The summer's ended? Life is dull and cold—
The heav'ns look gloomy grey—one spot alone
(To our sad fancies) on the dreary earth
Seems bright with sunbeams—even that hallowed mount,

Whereon of old the gracious lips proclaimed
A blessing on the mourner!   Our wan eyes
Strain towards it thro' their tears, as though thereon
They might ev'n now behold Him, the Beloved,
The world's great Comforter, in light enthroned
Breathing forth consolations, speaking peace
To all perturbed and sorrow-laden souls.
Thou Royal City! where uprose of yore
The Golden Temple gorgeous in the sun,
Now in the " Wailing Place " thy children sit,
And moan thy beauty and their glory gone!
Above thy yellow garland-wreathèd walls
The minarets, glitt'ring in the clear blue air,
Attest the Moslem sway o'er thee, thou tomb
Of martyr-prophets, proud Jerusalem!
Thy melancholy memories well accord
With Wilfred's pensive meditative mood,
As up the " Mournful Way " towards Calvary
He paces, learning patience at each step
From thought of One, who trod that way before.
A pilgrim to the city of the past,
In quest of peace and fortitude, he came ;
And while around him sounds of strife arose,
(Where Moslem, Jew, and Christian, " eye for eye "
And " tooth for tooth," still strive for mastery,)
He heard within the silence of his soul
The voice divine, that in the Temple courts
Announced the advent of the reign of love.

Beneath the shadowy archways, down among
The tombs by Kedron's stony bed, along
The lone ravine of Siloam's weed-grown pool,
He felt the presence of the " Blessèd One !"
Ling'ring at eve beneath the hoary trees
Of desolate Gethsemane, till rose
The yellow moon above the lofty ridge
Of Olivet, in fancy he could trace
The gentle Master's faintly-shadowed form,
Low bending 'neath the covert of the rocks,
In still communion with His Father, God!
In that yet lovely land of gardens, groves
Of orange and pomegranate ; where the vine
Hangs out its purple fruit, the white brier-rose
And graceful cyclamen grow wild, his heart
Now opened to a world of grateful thoughts
And exquisite sensations.   On the plain,
Where once the city of the Palm-tree stood,
By Jordan's waters consecrate, he sought,
In pure and pious contemplation wrapt,
The spirit of the God-like Nazarene.

Meanwhile how fared it in the lone retreat,
Where Näamah and her loved Gabriel dwelt?
The yellow rays of parting sunlight shone
Thro' the thick-clust'ring orchard trees, and o'er
The quaint-cut garden walks ; the evening air
Stirred the tall rushes at the water's brink,

Sighed o'er the sleepy flowers, and wand'ring past
The cottage casement rose-embowered, awoke
Wild strains of wailing music, breathing through
Æolian strings. Upon the daisied bank,
That slopes down to the clear transparent pool,
The wedded lovers sat, their tempers tuned
Accordant with the stillness of the hour.
A mournful shade on Gabriel's brow had fallen,
Unmarked by Näamah, till with a sigh
He broke the long dead silence, and thus spoke,—
" How this poor life of mine doth run to waste,
Bearing no fruit of all the days and years
I have toiled on, aspiring! hope was mine,
To sing one song at least of love and truth,
Ere my lips close for ever. Oh, to leave
Some sign, however feeble, just to show
That we have been! that we have loved and wept,
And sinned, and been forgiven, and sinned again,
Frail. loving, suffering souls, such as we see
Living and dying round us every day!
Thus to live after life, perchance be loved
By some sad lonesome spirit kin to ours,
To draw forth drops of pity warm and bright
From gentle eyes, or wake in worldlings' breast
Thoughts of some friend long lost, or early love
(Grateful and soul-reviving as a breath
Of cool sweet-scented wind to burning brow
Of pilgrim in the desert) such, (so far

Above my powers, ambition bade me soar!)
Such my fond hopes have been ; but I shall die,
And my frail bark in its brief course will stir
No ripple on the surface of the sea.
Sleep, weary longings, that wear out my life!
Regrets, that feed like cankers on my heart,
Impatient strife with doom! have I not learned
The lesson of my utter nothingness?
Stumbled in darkness, and stretched out my arms
Child-like towards the Parent Infinite,
And prayed some angel power might bear me up
From the black chaos where I grope in vain,
And place my weary feet on heights serene,
Where God's broad daylight shines eternally!"
How sunk her heart within her, as he spoke!
Fond Näamah, to deem thy woman's love
Could be to him all his love is to thee!
Thou learn'st the humbling lesson, which thy sex,
All, soon or late, must learn—that love, which makes
Thy sum of life, is but a part of his.
Thy hope, thy faith, thy very being tend
Towards him, its centre ; all thy soul's desires
By him are bounded—his are infinite—
Unresting—lost in the unseen, unknown.
" Still murmuring! still regretful!" answered she ;
" Earth must be void indeed of fair and good,
So soon to disenchant thee! few and brief
Thy years have been.   Oh, Gabriel! oh my love!

Dost thou regret the gladsome days of old ?
Deemest thou wedded life faint recompense
For thy lost freedom ? if I weary thee
With my excess of fondness, I will sit
Patient all day, nor ever move my lips
To say ' I love thee.'   I will fix my eyes
On the dull earth, nor raise them once to meet
Thy looks, which are to me as morning light,
As the first flush of spring, or whatsoe'er
Most welcome is, and cheering !   I will die —
Pass from thy memory, and leave thee free
To choose another friend, rather than live
And be to thee no more as I have been !"
E'en as she spoke, ere answer might be given,
With hasty footsteps rustling among the grass
A messenger arrived, most welcome guest !
Bringing glad news of absent friends and home.
And, dearer still, a letter from the East,
From the loved wand'rer, Wilfred.   With a cry
Of joy, upstarted Gabriel from the ground,
Pressed it all eager to his ardent lips,
And brake the seal.   How fondly Näamah
Watched his eyes brighten, and his pale cheek glow
Delighted, as he read : " Oh, blessed hour !
Thrice-blessed letter, fraught with happy news !
Most blest the hand, that penned it !   Näamah,
Rejoice ! no more from henceforth to be sad !
Moved to more gentle thoughts by Wilfred's prayers,

Our father pardons, welcomes us once more
To the old home, there with him to await
And greet my brother. after long delay
Ev'n now bound homeward. I shall see his face!
Hear that dear voice of his! press his warm hand!
Clasp him once more—my Wilfred! friend of friends!
Beyond expression excellent and dear!
Lift up thine eyes, sweet wife! Ah, dost thou weep?
Tears of delight! Yet weep not, lest they bring
To mind sad thoughts: for I have seen such drops
Too oft in sorrowful seasons on thy cheek,
To see them start unmoved at hour like this."

See Wilfred now, from shores of Palestine,
After his weary absence, bound for home!
'Twas afternoon, and some brief hours must bring
Once more the wand'rer to his native land.
He leaned against the ship-side, lost in thought.—
The sea was lulled, and hushed the winds awhile.
Impatient longing had outstripped the hour,
And wafted him in fancy to his home.
His father's voice already welcomed him—
And Gabriel's smile—and Naamah's fond eyes.
He saw them all before him as of old—
His brother's arm close-locked in hers (*his* wife
That should have been)—" Ah, me! what pangs are
        these
That shoot along my heart, and shake my frame?

E

What! can the ghost of buried love arise
After its long death-sleep to torture me?
Oh, mother, I am weary of this strife!
In my glad dawn of youth, thou know'st my prayer
Was still for 'love'—sweet 'love:' but times are
          changed,
This life is all too sad—my heart is sick—
My prayer is now for 'rest!'"   A breath of wind
Blew soft and cool across the young man's brow—
And cleared the air—and crept along the sea,
Whose mournful murmur low responded, " Rest."

     Meanwhile a crowd of glitt'ring guests were met,
To bid him welcome to his father's halls.
Light streamed from the tall casements, and the sound
Of music from within on the night wind
Was wafted to far distance—heard perchance
With wonder, 'twixt the pauses of his dream,
By some toil-wearied traveller, asleep
On couch of heather by the lone road-side.
The costly halls with countless lustres shone,
And the broad mirrors many a radiant group
Reflected of fair dames and maidens gay,
(With flutt'ring garments and pearl-wreathèd hair,)
And forms of stately lords, and knights, who paid
Due homage to the lovely and the young.
Rare perfumes from the orangery stole
On the delighted sense—mingled by turns

With scent of heliotrope and lilies faint,
Wafted thro' the open casement from beneath,
Where, as the clouds passed fitful o'er the moon,
The garden half in light and shadow lay.
Ne'er scene enchanted of Arabian Tales
More gorgeous showed—nor Houri, seen in dreams
By love-lorn Moslem poet, might compare
With Näamah, in robes of silken gauze,
The white rose and the blue forget-me-not
Twined in the wavy tresses of her hair,
Smiles on her lip, dimpling her dainty cheek,
And sparkling in her eyes;—such eyes! so soft,
And dark, and deep, you might for ever peer
Into their orbs, and yet not reach the depths
Of thought and love within them! Oh, to hear
Her bird-like voice ringing with laugh and song!
Mark the light motions of her fairy form!
You would have thought, that earth had changed its hues,
That pain and grief had never, ne'er could touch
So delicate a creature! Yet so like
Her own sweet self methinks she scarcely seemed
Amid earth's tinsel shows and vanities,
As when her daily duties she fulfilled
In simple garb, with sober cheerful mien,—
One, to whom life at once was grave and bright.
And Gabriel, where was he? from side to side
She cast her longing looks in search of him,
Turned at each sound of steps behind her own

In expectation to behold his face,
Beaming delight upon her. Wrought at last
To vague forebodings at his long delay,
And urged by yearning love, from out the throng
Of dazzling guests she passed, and swift as light
Above, below, by winding galleries sped
Thro' empty-sounding chambers, calling him
In chiding tones distressful, pausing oft
Deluded by the echoes, many-toned
That rung around—" Alas, why lingers he ?"
Fears and misgivings straight begin to rise,—
Her free step faltered, and a mist of tears
Clouded her sight, when, hark ! a welcome sound
Of feet approaching !—that impetuous tread
She knew full well, and in a moment more
Her Gabriel stood before her, with flushed cheek,
And fixèd look, like one that walks in sleep,
Peopling the air with phantoms of his brain.
" Ah, wherefore meet we thus ? is this thy love ?"
She cried in plaintive tones ; " At such an hour,
When, of thy presence reft, life's pulses beat
With faint and joyless motion thro' my frame,
And all bright scenes look pale and lustreless
To my dimmed eyes ?   Ah, speak ! what evil chance
(For such it needs must be, not thy neglect)
Hath robbed me thus of thy loved company ?"
Startled at sight of her, the colour fled
From Gabriel's face, leaving it mortal pale.

He shuddered faintly—glanced around, as though
By fearful memories disquieted—
Then spoke in hurried tone and tremulous:
" Oh, Näamah, I fear some evil doom
Hangs o'er our house! the clouds are gathering round,
Making night black without. Hour after hour
I watched upon the chapel tower for sign
Of sail upon the sea, some token sure
Of Wilfred's coming. Sick with hope deferred,
The air grown chill, at length I hasted down
And made towards the house. Slow drawing near
In the grey dusk, beneath the southern porch,
Surprised I saw my brother, arm outstretched
In act to pluck the Passion Flower (even so
I saw him once before) ; with cry of joy
I darted forth to clasp him in my arms,
When all at once he vanished!—Well I know,
Such fancies bode not good!—and oh! so like
The vision seemed — I could have sworn 'twas he !"
—" Thou troubled dreamer, cast thy fears aside !"
Said Näamah,—" Ere long will Wilfred's self
Be here to laugh at thy dark auguries!
Are these fit looks of greeting ? clear thy brow,
And ev'n for love's sake look thyself again !
Ah, gladden with thy presence this poor heart,
That pines without thee! Paradise itself
Would seem a barren waste, of thee bereft !"

The night grew dark and darker,—winds arose;
Storm-threatening signs appeared from time to time ;
A gradual chill crept thro' the festive hall,
Filling all hearts with doubt and sad surmise,
Till with grave looks, and farewells mute, the guests
Dispersed, ere the first stroke of midnight tolled.
At length with awful crash the thunder broke !
The rain came down in torrents! wrestling winds
Shook the strong house, and tore the aged trees,
While forkèd lightning, arm of quiv'ring fire,
Brought blast and desolation far and near.
The old Lord, trembling, to his chamber went,
To plead with Heav'n in terror for his son.—
The servants, awe-struck, in the upper rooms
Crowded, to watch the issue of the storm.
Within the porch, all silent, Gabriel stood —
His arm clasped Näamah's;—his eyes were raised,
As fain to pierce the darkness, and discern
Some trace of pitying Providence beyond.
" Why start you, love ?" low whispered Näamah,
And, shudd'ring, closer to her husband clung.
" I heard a sound as of distress at sea !
Hark! there again !—Hold, Näamah, thine hand !
Thou shalt not stay me !"—All in vain she urged,
'Twas but the thunder rolling up from far ;
In vain with frantic love she clasped him round,
With one strong wrench he tore him from her grasp,
And ere the cry of anguish broke, was gone,

Lost in the chaos of the storm without.
Long anxious hours unhappy Näamah
The desolate chambers paced, until the lights
Sunk flick'ring to their sockets, and died out.
She wandered up and down the hall, the stairs,
And corridors, like some remorseful ghost,
That could not rest. The wreath, that bound her hair,
Now shed its faded rose-leaves o'er her neck,
And down her snow-white vest:—a living corpse
Unearthly fair, with flowers for burial strewn,
She seemed.—Ah me! less piteous to behold
Was Jephtha's child amidst her weeping maids
Upon the mountains, where she silent sat,
Wan, anguish-stricken, Desolation's self,
Bewailing her stern doom, while balmy winds
Swept sighing past her with a mournful sound,
And o'er her raiment and her raven hair
The glist'ring dew-drops shone like angels' tears.
Will it ne'er end? the dismal night?—it moves
With leaden pace, and long ere morning breaks,
The storm is lulled, the raging winds abate,
And thro' the opening clouds faint moonlight streams
Athwart the marble pavement of the hall,
Silvers the cold white images around,
And sheds its lurid melancholy beams
Upon the Magdalen of sculptured stone.
Behold the sorrowing genius of thy house!
Weeps it not with thee, Näamah? the tears

Are frozen on its cheek! excess of grief,
And humbleness, and patience, is expressed
In that pale face; those downcast eyes, that gaze
Unutterably tender, full of trust,
Upon the blessèd emblem of the cross.
Misfortune's child, rest thou thine own thereon!

The day was dawning faintly:—wearied out,
Within an upper chamber on a couch
At length poor Näamah in slumber sunk.
But rest was not for her:—ere long the tramp
Of strange and hurried footsteps startled her.
She strove to still the beatings of her heart,
And held her breath, and listened eagerly.
Oh, direful moments of suspense! they came
Yet near and nearer,—up the avenue—
Along the terrace,—gained the vestibule.—
Low-murmuring voices reached her from beneath:—
She clasped her hands,—"'Tis he! 'tis Gabriel!"
Sprung from the couch, and, light as wingèd Love,
Sped down the stairs, and stood within the hall.

'Twas thronged with faces strange,—that seemed
        to her
Like faces in a dream:—she paused awhile,
Perplexed and speechless,—then, with eager air
And sense of chill heart-sickness, forced her way
Among the crowd, that in the centre stood,

And sudden saw, with eyes incredulous,
Close at her feet, upon a bier outstretched
The corpse of Wilfred : — ah, how pale he looked !
How calm, and fair, and stately in his death !
His dark brown dripping locks in tangles fell,
Leaving his forehead bare, and eyes, whose lids
The sea's soft kiss had sealed for evermore.
One cold dead hand hung down, and touched the ground ;
The other — locked in Gabriel's, who lay
Half fainting on the floor, with fallen head
Upon his brother's breast — a woful sight,
Almost as deathlike as the dead itself !

See, father, where he lies, thy beautiful son !
Dear witness of thine early halcyon days,
Thro' childhood, boyhood, youth, from first to last
Of his short life, all thy fond soul could wish !
Sons, that have wrung their parents' hearts with grief,
Brought desolation to the peaceful hearth,
Thronged with blithe faces ; — fouled their once fair
     names
With deep-dyed incradicable stains, —
Guilt-branded outcasts — such — live on, and drain
The very dregs of miserable life ;
While thy good son — thine aged heart's delight —
Thy first beloved, — thy friend, — thine all in all,
In youth's full prime lies lifeless at thy feet !
Weep not so sorely ! — what, if those dear eyes

No more shall meet thine own in filial love !
Those closed lips answer not thy piercing cry
Of lamentation ;—he is still thy son !
A crown of honour to thy hoary head !
As near to thee in death,—part of thyself,—
As in the hour of joy, when first he lay
Clasped to thy breast.   Not for a season God
Gave thee him, but for ever ! if awhile
He hide thy treasure from thee, patiently
Resign it to His keeping, nor believe,
Because thou seest it not, 'tis less thine own !

THE PASSION FLOWER.

PART III

" How wonderful is life ! from first to last
A mournful, hopeful, awful mystery !
Then, wherefore we (who know that nothing here
Is as it seems, and daily, hourly mocked
By outward semblances, mistake, misjudge,
And backward read the all-beneficent laws
That rule creation), wherefore should we deem
His absence, as it were, some grievous ill
Inflicted but to torture us in vain ?
All sights deceive us ! that which is most fair,
And most unlovely to corporeal sense,
Alike illusion ! Oh, if hill and stream,
Sunshine and tempest, glorious human forms,
And flowers—beloved with love of living things—
And the blue skies themselves, which we call Heav'n,
Are not as we conceive them, just it were
To deem, that mortal life, and pain, and death,

Are but disguises worn by some great good,
That hides a blessing in a seeming curse.
I do believe, behind the murkiest cloud
There is an angel's face,—aye, and a voice
Of love and pity in the thunder's roar,—
And in the loss of him, that was so dear,
And brave, and beautiful, a loftier gain
To him and us, than our poor hearts, pent up
In this obscure abode, can dream or guess!
Then, Gabriel, lift thine eyes, and look on her,
To whom the sight of thy despair doth make
This life a desolation! See, the sun
Yet pours its beams on this bereavèd earth!
All is not lost, while loveliness and love,
Howe'er despoiled, are left—and more than these
Sustaining thoughts of Christ, and prayers, that bring
The angels down of patience and of peace."

He hears not her sweet voice. With drooping head,
And listless arms down hung, and glassy eyes
That gaze on vacancy, for days he sat
A living form, forsaken of its soul.
Beside him Näamah, disconsolate,
Knelt, gazing on him with beseeching looks,
And called him by a thousand tender names,
And leaned her head against his heart, and sighed,
The saddest sigh e'er parted human lips.
Oft would she lift his motionless cold hands,

And fold them in her own, and fondly strive
To warm them with her kisses and her tears.
But all was vain to rouse him; till, at length,
It chanced, his father (who for years had nursed
A strange indifference to his youngest son),
Perceiving his sad plight, with wistful looks
(While tears ran down his cheeks) drew near, and laid
His furrowed hand 'mong Gabriel's golden curls.
A ray of love illumed the young man's face.—
He looked up with a transient smile, and leaned
His pallid cheek against his father's breast.
"Stay by me, father: I so love to feel
Thy hand upon me, hear thee call me 'son!'—
God knows, I cannot fill his place that's gone,—
Yet bear with me awhile, and when I die,
Remember not how wayward I have been,
How all unworthy;—but, oh, think of me
As one, who loved thee meekly, silently,
And prized thy love above all earthly things!"

Days, weeks, and months were numbered—but no
    more
The flush of health returned to Gabriel's cheek.
A melancholy calm possessed his soul,
Unnatural at his years, and with the hopes
He might have cherished still of life and love.
He sat with Näamah on summer days
Beside the porch, or near his brother's grave.—

And tho' she sang to him, and wearied not
To win him from his grief by mute appeals,
And prayers, and numberless endearing ways,
And womanly devices,—never more
His once so buoyant mood revived,—the hopes,
The cares of earth, had died out in his heart,
By mem'ry of his brother all absorbed.
" Mourn not for me, loved Näamah," he said,
" The strife has lasted long, but now I rest.
It was a fearful time when Wilfred died;
I scarcely can recall its agony,
And how I writhed beneath the stroke of doom!
I used to long for night, such hope I had,
That in the darkness I might see his face.
I called his name, and prayed him come to me
But for one moment—once again to look
On those beloved lineaments.   Alas!
How vain such expectation, to discern
With bodily eyes of spiritual semblance aught,
Reversing nature's all-wise law, that suits
Our senses to the sights and sounds alone
Of this material earth, denying us
A glimpse beyond; and tho' the spirit-world
Be all around, far nearer than we deem,
'Tis only death can rend the fleshly veil
That blinds us, and disclose it to our view.
In this probationary state how just,
That we should learn the lesson patiently

It hath to teach us, taking as they come
Or good or ill, for ill itself is good
That-is not guilt-entailed, but is from God.
I therefore am content to trust and wait :
Assured that He, in His best time, will lift
The scales from off my spirit's eyes, and change
This mortal darkness to immortal light."
Sore wept poor Näamah. " No more!" she said ;
" I cannot bear it now — so mournful strange
And ominous thy tones ! so like the knell
Of dying love ! Alas ! how thou art changed
From thy so lovely self of former days !
Thy brother in his death did steal thy heart
From all that once possessed it, making us
Mere abjects, of our only treasure reft.
Art thou thus eager to be gone ? to leave
Thy poor companion ? dost thou think to find
In other worlds a love more true than mine,
Who, ere I left thee lonely in thy griefs,
Had bartered half the blessedness above ?"

" Nor yearnings, nor resistance," answered he,
" Can change, dear heart, th' unchangeable ! I feel
The hand of doom is on me. Never think
I am not loath to leave thee ! art thou not
Heart of my heart, my life of life, my heav'n,
As thou wast ever ? thou didst make this world
Only too pleasant and too dear to me

And oh! when I am parted from thy side,
And thou dost weep—alas! I know thou wilt!
Let thy sweet heart take comfort in the thought,
That Death, so dreaded distant, drawing near
Breathes on the soul with effluence divine,
Until the atmosphere around is fraught
With sense of peace unutterably sweet,
Beguiling us so gently out of life,
That unawares we find ourselves in heav'n.
I know my end is near—last night I saw
Once more my brother standing in the porch,
With hand towards the Passion Flower upraised.
He gathered it for me: it is the flower,
That all the angels in their bosoms wear,
Since Christ's tears fell upon it, as He bowed
His head in anguish at Gethsemane."

" Ah, fold me to thy heart once more —once more —
Let me die with thee, Gabriel! should there be
No heav'n, no life to come, and we must lie
Inanimate clods, slow crumbling into dust—
All the sweet memories of our life, like stars,
Gone out for ever— all our tender love,
Our joys, and sorrows, wishes, hopes and prayers,
Become a blank, as tho' they ne'er had been —
Tho' nature, and this wonderful fair world,
Which we so dear have loved, no token keep
Of our brief frail existence—I fear not

To go with thee into eternal night!
To be as thou art, whatsoe'er thou be —
Nothing, if thou art nothing! even this
Rather than life without thee, which were death
In its worst shape — despair accompanied!
Wherefore should health thus glow throughout my frame,
While thine droops hourly? and my pulse beat strong,
While thine is faint? Alas! thy lips are pale!
The flush is fading from thy cheek! not yet —
I cannot yet part with thee, my soul's love!
Still strain me close and closer to thy breast —
Death shall not have the heart to part us thus!"

Mysterious, silent death! whose unseen touch
Transforms this vivid, soul-expressive frame
Into a wax-like image, cold as stone,
Inimitably pale and motionless:
A somewhat, that doth seem to appertain
Neither to earth nor heaven! — not terrible,
Yet awful to behold! the sight of thee
Doth teach us, — more than all the books e'er writ, —
And certify (as tho' attested audibly
By voice of God) that this corporeal shape,
— So wonderful and delicately wrought —
Is but the garment, which we wear on earth.
Turn, Näamah! ne'er hang upon that lifeless clay,
As thou wert grown to marble clasping it!
It cannot see thee — hear thee — answer thee! —

It is not Gabriel, more than are the clouds,
That sometime veil the sun, the sun itself.
Seek him henceforth in the still air around —
Among the flowers, and all sweet things he loved :
Believe him close beside thee, in the haunts
Of happy days departed : wheresoe'er
Is nature's aspect lovely and serene,
Thou likeliest art the influence to feel
Of his blest spirit breathing love on thine.
Peerless he was! ev'n from his birth endow'd
With heav'nly gifts.   As some rare fragile plant.
Torn from more genial soil, may haply bloom
While summer lasts : but, when bleak winds set in,
Is nipped and blighted, — his frail flower of life
Expanded in the warmth of hope and love,
But when chill sorrow touched it, shrank apace,
Waxed wan, and withered.   Even as thy gain
In love like his was great, so, Näamah,
Thy grief is in its loss!   Seek where thou wilt,
Thou canst not find another Gabriel!
Nor if, methinks, one charming past compare —
Fair as Endymion, when the goddess first
Eyed him with looks enamoured — eloquent,
Gentle and wise, should seek thy love to win
With promises of life's most rare delights,
Wouldst thou one moment swerve from loyalty
To thy dead love, more lovely to thy thoughts
(Ev'n in his garb of frail humanity)

Than the first angel of the highest sphere.
For love like thine, true love, (which in this world
Of counterfeits and falsehoods, is as rare
As true religion, or aught else of truth)
So hallows, elevates, and sanctifies
The image at its shrine, encircling it
With radiance mystical, that, as a veil,
Conceals its natural semblance, and, apart
From grosser idols worshipped for a day,
In the heart's "Holy of Holies" hides it safe
With thoughts of God associate — such true love
Can neither change with time, nor die with death!
Whoe'er would lure an angel down to dwell
In mortal tenement, must people it
With fit associates for such heavenly guest:
And who aspires true love to entertain —
God's love — our pledge of immortality —
Must beautify the temple of his heart
With store of wisdom, gentle thoughts and good,
And amiable affections: — faith and peace
And all the virtues must inhabit it: —
So it may seem a mansion fair, and meet
For that celestial visitant, — too pure
To breathe infected air, too bright to dwell
In dark abode with spirits base and foul.

Now hope had well-nigh died in Näamah, —
But that the Great Good, which is still most near

When needed most. in this her strait extreme
Let in a flood of glory thro' the gloom —
And gave her heart new lease of life and love
In that most wondrous gift of gifts — a child.
Mysterious messenger of promise! late
In fellowship with angels! Mystic sense
Of rev'rend awe athwart the rapture steals
Of thy impassioned mother, as she cons
Thy tiny form so wonderfully framed,
And smiles exultingly to find thy hand,
Tho' ne'er so small, can clasp her finger round.
O bliss undreamed! no more is Gabriel dead!
He lives in this his son, — soul of his soul, —
That will grow up to look, and move, and speak.
And grace the earth, ev'n as its father did!
" O, my child's soul, in thy mysterious course
From th' unimagined regions whence thou art,
Perchance thy father's spirit breathed on thee!
His love encircled thee, even as now
My feeble arms! Perchance he bade thee bear
Some token of his pity and his love
To thy bereavèd mother! O my child,
Couldst thou but speak! or I might kiss thy lips,
And find it there, or read it in thine eyes,
Or hear it in the murmurs of thy sleep,
'Ere earthly influences quite wear out
Its impress on thee!" As a link new wrought
Between herself and Heav'n this infant seemed

To Näamah,— Day-star, that ushered in
Her soul to land of promise! Nor brooked she
One moment from her jealous arms to part
The precious burden : morning, noon, and night,
Its presence was as influence divine —
Refreshing — renovating. 'Twas a joy
Too exquisite to last : and Näamah,
(While strangers shook the head with boding sigh)
In her blind passion, heeded not how frail
The thread, to which that little life was hung.—
Not till, with pallid lips and languid eye,
The babe lay stretched upon its fever bed,
Moaning in its unquiet sleep,— quailed she
Before the omens of impending doom :—
Not till the breath had ceased to warm its lips,
Its tiny heart to beat, and small hot hands
Grew damp within her own, could hope forego,
That this last overwhelming agony
Might yet be turned aside. Ah, who
Can speak her ultimate despair,— who paint
In living colours what she was,— how looked,—
How moved,— how lived,— and died not underneath
The weight of such accumulated woes ?
Crushed down by the sore anguish, days she lay
Unconscious of aught round her,— like to die :
Oft in delirious wand'rings courting death,
And calling on the dead with cravings wild
To draw her after them,— a grievous time!

But when the sickness waned, and she awoke
To sense of outward things, and saw once more
This beautiful earth in all its spring attire,—
The trees and lawn in earliest emerald green,—
And felt warm sunshine everywhere,—it seemed,
That Nature wore the old enchanted look
It used to wear; and her once ardent love
Returned for birds, and flowers, and all sweet sounds,
That thrilled her now with meaning deep and strange,
Like voices echoing from the angel-world.

The clods were green beneath the chapel wall,
Where Gabriel and his infant son were laid.
Beside them Wilfred and his mother slept—
All one in life, not parted in their deaths.
There scarce was spot in all the world so still!
The insects' buzz, and waving to and fro
Of the tall, feathery, yellow-crested grass,
Were all the sounds that stirred its solitude.
The garden-walks were fragrant still with flowers,
And strewn in spring-time with the shell-like leaves
Of the pink chestnut blossom; the gold fruit
And clust'ring bells of the arbutus hung
Year after year upon their dark green boughs,
As if no change had fallen upon the place,
No footfall and no pleasant voice was hushed.
Alas! as one by one we drop away,
And in the places, where we once were known,

Are known no more, how feebly felt the void
Our absence makes,—how soon our very names
Become a memory, cherished silently
By those few hearts that loved us!—Earth blooms on,
Mourning not, heeding not the myriad dead,
Whose grave she is! All flesh is grass indeed!

Now ofttimes on the terrace might be seen
The old man, leaning on his daughter's arm,
Come forth with trembling steps to feel the warmth
Of the glad sun at noon. His rev'rend head
Was bowed with years and sorrows; but for her,
The tears, yet warm upon her cheek, had left
Unmarred its loveliness, and glanced her eye
With ever-varying meaning, as of old.
How tenderly she guided his weak steps!
How gently stroked the wrinkled hand, that lay
On her sustaining arm!—She would oft gaze
With fond, imploring looks into his face,
And smile her old bright smile, then weep to see
The old man feebly strive with quiv'ring lips
To smile in answer. It would almost seem
She had forgotten her own griefs, so much
Remembering his, and sorrowed more for him
And his dead sons, than for herself, and all
The world of love she lost in Gabriel.
So young,—so full of graces,—so bereft
Of all, that makes life precious!— Yet forbear

To pity her, ye prosperous! upon whom
The plenitude of earthly bliss is poured,—
Hope, recompensed affections, store of friends,
And home with fair and happy faces thronged!—
She would not give the memories of her past
For all your present joys! Her heart doth hold
Within itself a heav'n of lovely thoughts
And consolations,—all-sufficing faith,
That nothing is in vain, but shall reveal
In the unknown hereafter purposes
Of love and wisdom never deemed of here.
How happier far, like Naamah, to lose
The human semblance of the soul we love,
And know, that henceforth neither time, nor chance,
Nor change, nor life, nor death, can intervene
To part that soul from ours!—How happier far
Than (in this treacherous and uncertain world,
Where ofttimes dark and stormy evenings close
The mildest summer's day) year after year
To know no severance, but live on and love,
Till love perchance wear out, and the warm heart
Beat faint and dull to that same voice, whose sound
Once thrilled its pulses with keen ecstasy:
Or (poisoned at the core by venomed tongues
That envy, shame, and foul suspicion breed)
From cold estrangement grow to rancorous hate,
And scorn, and wrath, and vengeful lusts against
The object of its sometime passionate love

And slavish adoration.   Even so
Th' ignorant pagan tramples under foot
The idol, he once served on bended knees.
It is the living whom we 've ceased to love,
Not the belovèd dead, are lost to us.
By such high faith was Näamah upheld
In her extremest hour of agony :
And her life's sun, that seemed as it had set
In darkness on the day her loved ones died,
Rose on the morrow with more mellowed light,
But cheeringly as ever.   All bright things
And lovely, as divining her great need,
Combined to bless and soothe her, till the void,
Made in her heart by absent love, was filled
With sights and sounds of beauty and of peace,
And rare imaginings of future joys.
—The faint winds lingered round her,—fond to breathe
With freshening balm upon her fevered brow :—
The tiny waves of the vast slumbrous sea,
That sparkled in the sun with rainbow tints,
Crept towards her as in reverence, fain to kiss
Her feet or garment's fringe.   The very stars
Seemed to grow brighter, as she gazed on them—
And on the wings of birds that fluttered by
Between her and the deep blue vault of heav'n,
She felt, as if her Gabriel's spirit past
Joyous and free, and left upon the air
Silent, invisible tokens of his love.

Sweet dreams she had, wherein night after night,
She met him face to face, and heard him speak —
And (linked her hand in his) went wand'ring on
Thro' endless sunny paths and greensward ways,
While seraph music sounded in her ear,
And Christ with looks beatified arose,
And pointed upward to th' eternal skies.

Farewell, fair Näamah! thou hast fulfilled
Meekly thy destiny, hast borne the cross
Of *Him*, who now consoles thee with His peace!
Heaven's light is all around thee, and thy heart,
With hope renewed, as in its glorious spring,
Doth yet confess that " life is beautiful!"
See, where the ominous Passion Flower lies dead!
Hear the blest voices calling thee from far:
While starry-vested angels wait to bear
Thy sainted soul to some serener sphere!

THE IMAGE OF THE TRUTH.

O EARTH! how quickly all things sweet,
  All precious, pure, and bright,
When borne upon thy bosom, pale,
  And lose their sweetness quite!

O man! perverting all things good,
  Degrading all things great,
Interpreting the loftiest truths
  To suit thy low estate!

How quickly to the infant soul
  Thy breath a taint imparts,
And Saints have scarcely walked by thee
  With uncorrupted hearts!

When One at last, divinely good,
  To bless thy world was giv'n,
And teach, thro' lowliness and love,
  The nearest road to Heav'n,

'Twas felt, that God was come to earth,
  For man ne'er spoke as He :
But proud men scoffed, and scorned His law
  Of simple charity!

And when His face was seen no more,
  His friends and followers said,
" Lest men forget the truths He taught,
  And deem our loved one dead,

Now let us raise an Image fair,
  The likeness of His grace,
That we may still delight our souls
  By gazing on His face!—

And place it in the open plain,
  Where sorrowful and poor
May gather round, and rest beneath
  Its shadow evermore!"

They made the Image spotless white
  Of goodly marble stone,
And nought so fair before or since
  In all the earth was known!

But others came,—" And build," they said,
  " A temple for its shrine :
'Tis meet from vulgar gaze to hide
  An Image so divine!

And place a priest before the door
   To hear the pilgrims' prayer,
And grant them just a glance within
   Upon the glory there!"

Then, east and west, adorers came;
   And one with other vied,
Erecting each his separate shrine
   To Him, all deified:

Till round and round the sacred spot
   Innumerous temples rise,
And hide the Image in the midst
   For ever from men's eyes.

Some built of stone, some gold-inwrought,
   And on each front engraved,—
" Who seeks the truth elsewhere, is lost ;—
   Who seeks it here, is saved!"

Presumptuous boast! while none contains
   The Image pure and white,
And pilgrims roam from shrine to shrine
   In vain to find the right!

Yet know we, man nor time can change
   The ever-hallowed spot,
Where stands the Image of the **Truth,**
   Altho' we find it not!—

Tho' brave men have been, who have fought
  Thro' prejudice and pride
To find again that Image fair,
  And in the struggle died,

The veil shall yet be rent in twain,—
  The Holy Place revealed,
Where falsehood all too long has dared
  To keep the truth concealed!

THE WOODEN CROSS.

'Tis a little wooden Cross; —
  Nothing worth you see; —
Yet I love it very dearly,
  For he gave it me,

Long ago, in summer time :
  I was young and wild ;
He, a very saint in goodness,
  Brave, and wise, and mild.

" 'Tis a wooden Cross,—no more ;"
  Flatteringly he spake,—
" Yet I love you, take it, keep it
  For a poor man's sake !"

Ah, those lips so eloquent !
  I can see them now,
And the sudden glory lighting
  Up his cheek and brow !

Poor! yet he had made me rich!
    Love, from such as he,
Was a fitter gift for angel,
    Than for one like me!

On my neck he bound the Cross,
    Blessing me the while; —
Such a tender, mournful meaning
    In his voice and smile!

And I never saw him more,
    Never heard again
Tones, whose mem'ry still makes music
    In my heart and brain.—

It was well perhaps he died: —
    Better far to be
In the grave, methought, than suffer
    Half my misery!

But the Cross, the wooden Cross,
    On my bosom lay,
And I kissed and wept upon it
    Twenty times a day:

Till there came the thought of Him,
    Sufferer divine!
Unto whose great weight of anguish,
    What were griefs like mine?

And a quiet, strange and sweet,
   O'er my being stole,
 Like the breath of some good angel
   Passing o'er my soul.

Years of pain, how quickly sped!—
   Near my grave I stand,
Straining thro' the misty evening
   Toward the spirit-land!—

Lay the Cross upon my breast,
   When in death I lie;—
Do not break the spell, that binds it
   To my destiny!

Emblem of my hope and love,
   Balm to soothe and save,
Let me take my treasure with me
   To the grave!

CHRIST.

Tho' the joys, that now delight thee,
Faint may wax and tame,
I am still the same.
Tho' the hearts, that say they love thee,
Turn to cold and strange,
I can never change !

Tho' the hopes, that cheer thy spirit,
Pass like shadows frail,
Mine can never fail.
Tho' thy bosom's best affections
Wrong and falsehood sever,—
Mine endure for ever !

Tho' life's promise disappoint thee,
All thy toil and pain
Spend themselves in vain,—

Tho' the world look coldly on thee,
Spurn, and scorn thy faith, —
I am true till death!

Tho' it leave thee tossed and shipwrecked
On a stranger land,
I am still at hand :
Come, thou poor, forsaken one,
By grief and wrongs oppressed,
" I will give thee rest!"

Am not I the " Rock of Ages ?"
Found thy faith on me,
That cannot moved be :
Then let all the powers of darkness
Seek to bruise and break thee,
I am with thee, oh, believe me,
" I will never leave thee,
Nor forsake thee!"

THE ANGEL OF LOVE.

On noiseless wing, one starry night
    From her blest home above
Down, dove-like, came that Angel bright,
    Whose care is human Love.

A rose upon her bosom lay,
    Fresh culled from Eden's bowers;
Unlike the rose, whose sweets decay
    On this sad earth of ours.

Within its cup is found a balm
    For love's severest pain;
Desponding hearts to raise and calm,
    And give them hope again.

Where Jordan's tranquil waters shine
    Beneath the sun's warm rays,
Two sisters fair of Hebrew line
    Had passed their quiet days.

In mutual love and virtue blest,
　They scarce had dreamed of woe,
Till hopeless passion marred their rest,
　And forced their tears to flow.

Both loved, alas! a Christian knight,—
　Both shared an equal pain :—
For Christian vow no Jew may plight—
　They knew, they loved in vain!

Nor angry thought, nor envious strife,
　Stirred either gentle breast :
Each would have yielded love and life
　To make the other blest!

The gracious Angel was not slow
　Those sisters' griefs to feel,
Nor ever wept for human woe,
　She did not strive to heal.

The sisters watched in speechless dread
　Her radiant shape appear :
" Fear not; my name is Love," she said ;
　" And peace my mission here.

No sigh, how faint, how sad soe'er,
　Is heard in vain on high :
A balm of power divine I bear
　To soothe and sanctify.

To her, who loves with deepest love,
　　This flower of life be given;
It has been reared by saints above,
　　And bathed in dews of Heaven."

The Angel to the elder spake;
　　" What canst thou, wilt thou, do
Or bear for thy beloved one's sake,
　　To prove thy love is true?"

" Oh, doubt it not," the maiden cried:
　　" All joys would I resign,
So I were sometimes at his side,
　　And dared to call him mine!

My father's land, my sister's home,
　　Mine ancient creed forego,
With him on distant shores to roam,
　　And share his weal and woe!

No other bliss below, — above, —
　　No other hope be given!
Life were not life without his love,
　　And, with it, earth were heaven!"

The Angel to the younger spake:
　　" What, maiden, wilt thou do
Or suffer for thy loved one's sake,
　　To prove thy love is true?"

"I love him well," the maid replied;
  "And much would I resign,
To be for ever at his side,
  And know his heart was mine.

My father's creed is dearer yet,—
  Mine ancient race and name:
Then break my heart, ere I forget
  The Israel, whence I came!

Yet tho' my vows I may not break
  To share his happier fate,
To deeds of love, for his loved sake,
  My days I consecrate.

No other love this heart shall share,
  To his for aye consigned;—
No thought of evil enter, where
  His image is enshrined!

But I the sick and poor will tend,—
  My life an offering make
In trust, that Heaven on him may send
  A blessing for my sake!"

The Angel smiled: "The Rose is thine:
  Such love is love indeed:
So love,—so live: and love divine
  Eternal be thy meed!"

SPRINGS IN THE DESERT.

I PACE the long-deserted rooms,
  Still striving to recall
The sound of footsteps on the stairs,
  Or voices in the hall.

Along the walks, and up the lawn,
  I wander every day;
And sit beneath the mulberry's shade,
  Where most we loved to play.

No stir of feet the stillness breaks,
  No dear familiar tone,—
Since, taking each her separate way,
  They left me here alone.

To love them, and their love to share,
  Was life and joy to me;
I was the eldest of the house;
  My sisters, they were three.

As one, who marks the bud unfold
    A flower of radiant hue,
I marvelled day by day to find
    How beautiful they grew!

I knew them pure, and fit for life,
    If earthly life were given;
And oh, I knew, if they should die,
    They were as fit for heaven.

Our childhood was a merry time;
    And grief, if grief we knew,
Seemed only sent, like rain, to make
    The flowers spring up anew.

We parted; one to lordly halls
    In foreign climes was led:
Where love each day some new delight
    O'er her life's pathway shed.

The other chose a lowlier lot,
    A poor man's home to share,
To cheer him at his daily toil,
    And soothe his daily care.

The last and youngest,—where is she?—
    I thought she would have stayed
To talk with me of other days
    Beneath the mulberry's shade.

I loved her, as a mother loves,
　　And nightly on my breast
She laid her fair and gentle head,
　　And sung herself to rest.

I knew she could not find her peer
　　Among the sons of clay:
Yet how I wept, when angels came
　　To take my flower away!

And years have passed,—long silent years,—
　　Since first I dwelt alone
Within the old deserted house,
　　Whence so much love was gone!

I was not, like my sisters, fair,
　　Nor light of heart as they:
I always knew, that mine would be
　　A lowly, lonely, way.

But they, who deem my portion hard,
　　Know not, that wells are found
In deserts wild, whose silent streams
　　Make green the parchèd ground.

There's not a blade of grass,—a leaf,—
　　A breath of summer air,
But stirs my heart with love for *Him*,
　　Who made this earth so fair.

And many a lowly friend have I,
    Or sick, or sad of heart ;
Who hails my coming steps with joy,
    And sighs when I depart.

No day is ever long ; and night
    Some gentle spirit brings
To whisper thoughts of other worlds,
    And of diviner things.

And if, when evening shadows fall,
    I sad or lonely feel,
I kneel me down in that same room,
    Where we four used to kneel—

And there I say the ev'ning prayer,
    We four were wont to say : —
The very place hath power to charm
    All gloomier thoughts away

I have a thousand mem'ries dear
    And quiet joys untold ;
For God but takes His gifts away,
    To give them back tenfold !

THE SIBYL'S PROPHECY:

So fair a night was not, since Eve first slept
Beneath the stars in balmy Paradise.
All evil powers enchained in slumber lay —
While from the outspread wings of angels came
An holy influence down, awakening hope,
In sad and weary hearts, of some great good
Unknown, mysterious, dawning on the world!
Now hushed were all melodious sounds — no note
Of bird or insect's hum ; dead silence reigned
Through favoured Tempe's vale, save where the breeze
With fitful sighings stirred the trembling leaves.
The crispèd dew lay twinkling on the grass —
And the tall trees their clust'ring shadows cast
O'er Peneus' moonlit stream ; when by its shores
To wander forth a band of poets came.
Strange sense of awe, and expectation vague,

Filled all their hearts, and chained their tuneful tongues:—
They raised inquiring glances to the skies—
Now started, breathless, list'ning for the tones
Of fancied voices borne upon the wind
Or on the murmuring tide; when, lo! a sound
Of sweet strange music stole upon the air,
Like those wild melodies, which winds awake
Low breathing through Æolian strings.   They heard!
With one accord they hailed the gracious sound!
" It is the signal of the prophetess!
At yonder shrine she holds her midnight watch,
And summons us, her sons in sacred lore,
To hold, through her, communion with the skies."
With marble front, all glistening in the moon,
The solitary temple grandly stood,
Where never sound of tumult, mirth, or grief,
Disturbed the stillness consecrate to heaven.
There, 'neath its porch, her long dark locks unbound,
With aspect pale and wrapt, and starry eyes,
The Sibyl stood, and, as with rev'rend mien
The poet band approached, a radiant smile
Lit up her face with love and joy divine.
" Oh, Sons," she said, " and children of the light!
Have ye not heard strange whisp'rings in the air,
And rustlings as of footsteps 'mong the trees?
Seen in the moonbeams faces from the dead,
And felt within mysterious pulses throb
Through all your being? 'tis a wondrous night!

To-night this time-worn world is born anew!
A God takes human shape, and comes with power
Invincible, resistless, to subdue,
And purify, and elevate the earth!
The consummation of our blissful dreams,
The golden age revives, the age of peace!
All hail! thou chosen, best beloved of Heaven,
That shalt with thy philosophy divine
Convert mankind, and lift them to the gods!
Mighty regenerator! mightier far
In lowliness, than kings upon their thrones!
Mighty in life to love, and bless, and save—
Mightiest in death, that conquers all but thee!"
The Sibyl paused—her rapture-kindled eyes
Grew dim with tears, as if some sudden grief
Had chilled her heart: and with dejected tone
She thus resumed—"Oh, transports quickly past!
Oh, earth! what canker hides within thy heart
To taint all good, and blight the buds of hope?
Oh, man! what curse is thine, when Heaven itself
Shall fail to lift thee to diviner life?
The law of wisdom, innocence, and peace
(Bequest of Deity) is scarcely passed
Into men's hands, but strifes and discords rise,
And hate is kindled at the name of love!
Vain disputations, cavillings profane,
Displace heroic deeds, and lives sublime,
And make the holy Truth of none effect.

The followers of the godlike Lawgiver
In countless sects divide, and fill the earth
With wars and persecutions, scorn and hate,
Torture and death in every direful shape,
That heart of fiend conceives, or hell can frame.
Each deems itself supreme, and curses deals
On all beside, monopolising heaven,
And that free love, that yearns o'er all who live!
Oh, gentle Light! that through our darkness gleamed,
Art thou, then, quenched in blood?   Oh, soul of Love,
Has hate already driven thee from earth
Back to thy native seat among the stars?
Men know thee not—an Idol they have framed
In their own likeness (oh, how unlike thee!),
And called it Truth; an incoherent scheme
(After the fashion of their ignorance framed),
To mystify the mind and leave it void.
Thy consolations they have changed to threats,
Thy promises of life to fears of death;
For deeds of justice, piety, and ruth,
Are pomps, and feasts, and vain solemnities!
Th' undying spirit of thy Love, that seeks
An habitation in the human heart,
Wanders forlorn, dejected through the earth,
Or haunts the altar, where thy blood was spilt,
To mourn that such a sacrifice divine
Had not been offered for a worthier world.
Weep, gentle poets! aye, and gods will weep

To find so frustrated their high intents
Of charity to man.   Yet, all not lost;
For He who comes, Truth's grand Interpreter,
Shall found e'en yet His kingdom upon earth
Immutable, eternal as Himself.
A dazzling vision rises on my sight!
I see the golden portals wide unfold,
And crowds, all garlanded in vestments bright,
Are entering in.   From east and west they come,
Of every sect and nation under heaven,
The pure, and good, and true, from whose chaste lips
Nor curse nor slander fell : who lived in peace,
And on whose brows—His name (the Kingdom's King)—
Shines out inscribed in star-like characters!   ·

" Oh, haste ye, poets ! cast your bays aside,
For virtue henceforth wins the palm of fame !
Go, consecrate the flame divine to Him
From whom it emanates—the Eternal Good.
So ye among the chosen band may be
Unowned of men, but registered above
As champions for the kingdom of the Truth !"

HEAVEN?

QUESTION AND REPLY.

Oh rich man! 'mid the splendours of thy state
Uneasy still, still murmuring at thy fate,
With all, that earth can yield of rare and bright,
To charm thy soul, thy senses to delight,
For lack of labour languidly oppressed,
On couch voluptuous vainly courting rest,—
Untried by actual griefs, yet rarely free
From fancy's self-inflicted misery.—
What is that good,—thy far-off fond desire,—
That dream of Heaven, to which thy hopes aspire?

" Oh, whatsoe'er doth least resemble thee,
Thou dull and irksome earth, were heav'n to me!
Some distant world, where dreams of mortal bliss
Revive no more the memory of this,—
Its hollow shows,—vain mimicry of joy,—
Its pomps that sicken,—and its sweets that cloy!"

H

Oh! poor man, reared in squalor, gloom, and care,
For thee, life's bitter portion is to bear,—
To toil with wearied limbs for wages scant,
Yet still to hear thine infant's wail of want!
Racking thy heart, now glares, thro' the dim light
That face (how changed!) which once so cheered thy sight!
Death haunts thee in dire shape and grim despair,
At home, abroad, for ever, everywhere:
Yet even thou dost sometime lift thine eyes,
Straining with misty vision toward the skies:
Hast thou no vague, fond hope of some bright home
Reserved for thee and thine in worlds to come?

" Among the 'many mansions,' fair and blest,
Within our 'Father's house' I pray to rest!
Where equal bliss and equal honour wait
The rich and poor, the lowly and the great.
Where children's sobs no more my rest may break,
Nor hungry looks reproach me when I wake!
Where its young strength my spirit may regain,
And the dull load be lightened from my brain,—
And hearts, that here my cup of sorrow share,
Shall drink with me of joys immortal there!"

Thou, for the long-lost dead, that mournest yet,
On whose sad life the sun of love is set,
That sitt'st forlorn, abstracted,—with pale eyes
Feeding thy griefs on dreams and memories,

Thy Heaven 't will be to meet the looks once more,
To hear the voice, that charmed thy life of yore!—
Voice, that will welcome thee in rapturous tone,
To that blest land, where partings are unknown!

O sage! that fain beneath the midnight skies
Would solve the mystery of mysteries,
Unfold the secret, mighty and sublime,
Denied to man from immemorial time;
The Heaven for which thou yearnest is, to know
The past, the future,—all things, high and low—
Explore the myriad worlds, that round us roll,
And world as wondrous in the human soul,—
Pierce to the universal central sun,
Where, unapproached, dwells th' Eternal One!—
To such dread heights thy soaring soul aspires
In worship, winged with infinite desires!

Thou child of genius!—poet!—prophet!—seer!—
That with love-darting, dauntless eye dost peer
Into the depths profound of life and death,
What wondrous visions startle thee beneath?
Thy light of truth on life's illusions shine,
And teach us somewhat of the life divine!
Alas! ev'n thou canst yield no sure reply—
Thy falt'ring accents into silence die.
In vain has fancy soared, and reason striv'n
To gain some nearer insight into Heav'n,—

The wisest angel from the worlds of bliss
May teach us many things,—but oh! not this.
Yet know we, the Omniscient Good, (towards whom
We yearn thro' doubt and death's apparent gloom)
Had never given us sight of sun or star,
Faint glimpses of the myriad worlds afar,—
Vague hope of joys, which have no being here,
Were we not born to some diviner sphere!

CONSOLATOR.

Benoni, "son of sorrow,"—rightly named,
Thou orphaned, widowed, childless,—all bereaved!
Lift up thy drooping eyelids, swoll'n with grief,
From the ungrateful earth, that drinks thy tears,
And gives thee back but breathings of decay!
The beautiful gay spring is gone; the grass
All worn, and parched, and withered, thirsts for rain:
The crumpled, crumbling leaves fall noiselessly
Thro' the dead sultry air among the shrubs.
The white stock fades, and faint campagnola
Grows colourless, and droops for lack of dew.
The lark sings not, but the imprisoned dove
Coos to her mate complainingly, perchance
Lamenting her lost nest among the woods.
All nature mourns with thee, most desolate!
Too desolate to heed its sympathy,
Or aught beside thine all-engrossing griefs!
Thou art as one, to whom long since was giv'n

A garden, grown with plants of promise rare,
Exceeding delicate; and, doomed to see
Thy loveliest flowers, just bursting into bloom,
Uprooted one by one and flung aside,—
With wildered looks, despairing, impotent,
Stand'st gazing on the ruin at thy feet!
Oh, melancholy spirit of the past,
That haunts each scene familiar, peopled late
With living forms, and echoing to the tones
Of blessèd voices! Oh, thou tomb-like house,
The winds, that creep along thy panels, sound
Like phantom wailings o'er sepulchred joys!
The instruments of music, silent, rust;
And flowers, that decked the hall, are faded; cold
Fair hands that culled them!—On the wall still hangs
The picture of Christ's face;—methinks the eyes,
That glanced of old in mild admonishment,
Now beam thro' tears a tenderness divine!
Benoni, once so blithe, now smitten sore
With dearth of all love's wealth!—the good, the pure,
The beautiful are hidden from thine eyes!
What need of knell to help such souls to Heaven,
Or monument to boast in vulgar gaze
Their graces and thy griefs? or aught beside,
With which poor man deludes himself, in hope
To ease the wounds, that nothing here can heal?
This life is full of sorrow! Are we not,
"Sure as the sparks fly upward," born to weep?

When mother Eve first gazed in wonderment
Upon her eldest born, and fondly deemed,
That children to their parents' hearts must prove
Exhaustless source of comfort and delight,
She grateful named her infant—Cain, " a gift."
Too soon, by vigils early and late, by griefs
And crowding cares, her expectations found
All frail and vain ; and smarting with the pangs
Of disappointed hopes, what wonder she
Should call her next child—Abel. " Vanity!"
She erred, as err her children after her!
We have not heart to face our destiny
In its true colours,—fain would overlay
The prospect of our future with false lights
And rainbow hues inconstant,—till the storm
Breaks o'er the scene and sweeps them all away.
Earth holds worse woes than sorrow such as thine :
On all sides round thee Rachel's voice is heard.
See life-long ties dissevered, broken hearts,
That cannot brook the coldness of a friend,
Homes grown thro' discord hell-like,—happy hearths,
Where once sweet eyes looked love, made desolate
By sin and shame, that outlives life itself!
Hear the lorn mother's wail, that waits in vain
Her prodigal's return,—the bitter cry
Of souls awaked to consciousness of guilt,
That, maddened beyond human sufferance,
Rush headlong upon self-inflicted death!   .

Distracted hearts repeat the patriarch's plaint —
" Would I had died, ev'n in mine hour of birth,
Then had I quiet lain, and been at rest!"
So, will not we : Benoni ! lift thine eyes,—
Shake off thy trouble, clear thy sense, and note
The " still small voice," that rises in the east
From Nazareth's lowly valley, and floats on,
Eternal and melodious,— heard above
The whirlwind and the thunder, reaching out
To worlds and systems infinite,— beyond
Vibrating thro' the silences of space.
" Blessèd are ye that mourn ! come unto me,
Ye heavy-laden ! weep not for the dead,
That are not dead, but sleep and shall awake !—
Ah, fear not, little Flock, this world of death ;
For ye are mine, that am the Way, the Truth,
The Life ; and I the world have overcome!"—
The rain has fallen, and the earth revives :
The dripping branches of the trees are stirred
By evening winds, and thro' their leaves the sun
Shines warm and mellowed on thine eyelids wan.
See where the gold and purple heart's-ease springs
Close at thy feet, all filled with dew, like some
Dear faithful friend, that smiles on thee through tears !
Ah, gather up the fragments that remain
Of broken joys ! although life's treasure-house
Is much despoiled, the jewels snatched away
Shall be restored in twofold preciousness,

Or when or where we know not; as He wills
Who, (when the waves of this world's agony
Beat on our fragile bark of life, and nigh
Would overwhelm it,) walks in light
Upon the foaming waters, and uplifts
His voice Divine, " 'Tis I, be not afraid!"

ICHABOD.

"Oh, wherefore is my mother's face
So sad and wan?" I said:
And when she sighed, "Thy father, child!"—
I knew, that he was dead.

Upon her bosom, three months old,
My baby brother lay:
"And you must be his mother, child,
When I am called away.

The glory of my life lies low
Beneath the churchyard sod;
Then take my son, to sorrow born,
And name him Ichabod."

I took him from her dying arms,
And in my anguish cried,
"Love is the curse of life! of love
My gentle mother died!

I will not love, save this young child,
   This orphaned Ichabod;
And, as I give my heart to him,
   So give I his to God.

Nor dream of joy shall tempt us here,
   Where naught to last is given,
But all our thoughts, and hope, and love,
   Shall wing their way to Heaven!"

Years past,—I bore him in my arms,
   Till active, grown, and strong,
We played together in the fields
   With laughter, dance, and song;

And every night his little prayers
   He said beside my knee;
And oh, whate'er is best in life
   My brother was to me!

And when the seal of manhood first
   Was set upon his brow,
Upon the altar-steps he took
   Th' irrevocable vow,

And decked him in the priestly robe,
   And all his days consign'd
To bear the Cross of Him, who died
   In love to human kind.

So beautiful, so grand he stood
  In those too sanguine days ;
I sigh to think how proud I was,
  When all men spoke his praise !

What blessèd days in works of love
  And tranquil joy we spent,
Our hearts at peace with all the world,
  And with ourselves content !

At ev'n we walked beside the sea
  To watch the setting sun,
And breathe the fresh cool evening breeze,
  When all our toil was done.

Oh, wherefore, sorrow, didst thou take
  A form so frail and fair
To lay my pride with chast'ning low,
  And change it to despair ?

When first I marked her sweet sad face
  And meek uplifted eyes.
I took her for some messenger
  Of mercy from the skies !

The pomps of earth weighed heavily
  Upon a form so light,—
The daughter of an Earl was she,
  Betrothèd to a Knight.

Oh, fatal was the day, when first
    Across our path she trod,
For she was in her beauty's prime,
    And so was Ichabod!

And, free from guile, nor fear of sin,
    Nor danger marred their rest,
Till friendship's flame unconscious grew
    To love in either breast.

As blind I trusted in his strength,
    Till time its frailty proved,
So mad I writhed with grief and shame,
    When first I knew they loved.

Cold horror seized the luckless maid,
    Remorse and wild dismay,
To find her heart, unweeting, drawn
    Thus fearfully astray.

I knew the anguish of her soul,—
    But what was that to me?
I had nor pity, thought, or care,
    Save, Ichabod, for thee!"

The organ-tones had died away,
    The midnight mass was o'er;
I stood upon the altar-step,
    She knelt upon the floor.

Her forehead touched the marble stone,
　　Her hands were clasped in prayer:
The dying lamps threw fitful gleams
　　Upon her golden hair.

And as she raised her face to Heav'n,
　　So sad, and wan, and meek,
The Saints themselves had wept to see
　　The tears upon her cheek!

But I,—her cold hands crushed in mine,
　　I could have laid her dead!—
" Thou serpent in an angel's form.
　　God judge thy sins!" I said.

" He was the chosen of his Lord!
　　A seal was on his brow,—
But thou the temple hast profaned,
　　And laid his glory low!"

She clasped my knees.—" Oh. curse me not!"
　　With frenzied sobs she pray'd,
" But bid me live, or bid me die.
　　And thou shalt be obeyed!"

" Go, bid thy bridal guests," I said,
　　" And wed thine injured knight,
And hide thy fatal witcheries
　　For ever from our sight!"

Oh, lightly lay the morning dew
    On grass, and flower, and tree;
And softly crept the summer breeze
    Across the deep blue sea!

And village maidens, far and near,
    Brought wreaths and garlands gay,
To strew beneath the young bride's feet
    Upon her marriage day.

I saw the church with faces thronged,
    I saw the hapless maid,
A victim in her bridal robe
    For sacrifice arrayed!

I saw my brother's pallid lips
    Convulsive move in prayer:
His ashen brow and sunken cheek,
    And eyes, that looked despair!

I heard him seal with hollow voice
    The everlasting vow:—
"And God be thanked," I said, "his soul
    Is safe from evil now!"

I hurried from the fatal spot:
    I dared not stay to see
My idol humbled to the dust
    In silent agony!

I sat down to the bridal feast
   Within the castle wall :
But pale and silent were the guests,
   And gloom hung over all.

The bride upon her chair of state,
   Arrayed in gems of gold,
With front erect and fixèd look
   Sat speechless, calm, and cold.

They called her name, and chafed her hands,
   And loosed her jewelled vest;
But life nor lingered on her lip,
   Nor fluttered at her breast!

The guests shrunk back; the bridegroom raved
   Like one with grief gone wild;
The wretched father wrung his hands,
   And called upon his child.

We bore her to the bridal bed,
   And robed her limbs in white;
And thro' the darkened chamber lamps
   Were burning day and night.

We wreathed her brow with orange-flowers,
   With roses strewed her o'er,
Till mortal bride had never looked
   So beautiful before!

We knelt beside her grave and wept,
  " Thy will be done, O God !"
Then up I rose, and hurried home
  To comfort Ichabod.

I sought him high and low ; explored
  The empty house in vain ;
I called him in despairing tones ;
  He answered not again !

O'er hill, and dale, and moorland wide,
  Like some distracted ghost,
That never rests, in hope to gain
  The heav'n too early lost.

I wander'd, even to barren wastes,
  By human foot untrod,
And made the rocks and caves resound
  The name of Ichabod !

I paced the noisy city streets
  With weary foot and sore,
But no man asked me whence I came,
  Or oped to me his door !

The night was dark with wind and rain,
  Upon the bridge I stood ;
With rushing sound beneath me rolled
  The river's angry flood.

I saw the threat'ning clouds above,
　The threat'ning tide below:
"There is no refuge, God," I said,
　"Save death, to whom I go!"

Upon the verge of fate I hung,—
　When lo! a sudden gleam
Of moonlight thro' the darkness broke,
　And glistened on the stream!

And in its silver rays I saw
　The pale and lovely face
Of her, whom long ago I deemed
　A messenger of grace.

The flowers yet hung upon her robe,
　And wreathed her golden hair,
And lingered on her lips the smile,
　That holy angels wear.

I sunk repentant to the earth,
　And prayed in lowly plight,
That God would still be near my soul,
　And keep His Heav'n in sight.

"And I will seek thy grave," I said.
　"Thou monitress divine,
And tame my proud, rebellious heart
　To patience such as thine!"

'Twas evening, and the summer sun
    Was fading in the west ;
I stood among the low green graves,
    Where lay the dead at rest.

I marked the sculptured tomb, where death
    Long since received the bride,
And all o'ergrown with turf and flowers
    A lowly grave beside !

A marble Cross above it stood
    To guard the sacred sod,
And there with wond'ring joy I read
    The name of Ichabod !

I flung my arms about the Cross
    With tears and kisses vain,
As if the cold hard stone could speak,
    And answer me again !

" O thou, too much my crown of life !
    Thou Idol of my heart,
Too late upon thy grave I learn,
    How frail a thing thou art !

Too late deplore the cruel vow,
    That marred thy hapless past,
To curses all earth's blessings turned,
    And broke thy heart at last !

Presumptuous Priest! such vows profane
  The hallowed laws of God!
Bear witness many a blighted soul,
  Like my poor Ichabod!"

THE SHADOW OF THE HAND.

" How varied are life's flowery ways
   By varied pleasures strown !
But there, where Duty points the track.
   Is happiness alone ! "

Thus musing as. in fancy, far
   My footsteps seemed to stray,
Methought some strange mysterious power
   Impelled them on their way.

It was a shady path I trod,
   Yet beautiful to see ;
For there were flowers upon the turf,
   And birds in every tree.

I loved the flowers, their form, their hue.
   Their fragrance faint and rare ;
I loved the birds, whose pleasing strains
   Harmonious filled the air !

The clust'ring shadows of the trees
  Upon the ground were cast ;
They seemed to change their forms each time
  A breath of wind went past.

And, strange ! methought, as if the path
  Were some good angel's care,
The figure of a Hand I traced
  Among the shadows there !

A Hand, that ever pointed me
  Along that lonely way,
A way so happy, strange 'twould seem.
  That I should wish to stray !

Yet oft, too oft, I knew not whence,
  Gay sounds would meet mine ear
Of music, mirth, and revelry,
  And I would pause to hear.

And thro' the trees, on either side
  My shady path, would gleam
Bright eyes and glittering forms, such sights
  As happy lovers dream.

And they would call in wily tones,
  That sounded sweet and low,
And wave to me their snow-white arms,
  Until I longed to go !

But while that Shadow of the Hand
    Upon the greensward lay,
I could not turn to right or left,
    A charm was on the way !

I felt beneath that hallowed spell
    New life my being thrill,
And all things lovely seemed to take
    A lovelier semblance still !

The air breathed purer ; from the flowers
    A rarer fragrance given,
And thro' the leaves above I saw
    The blue and quiet heaven !

All was so sweet within that path,
    I could not from it stray,
Nor leave that Shadow of the Hand,
    Heav'n-sent to point my way.

There may be sunnier paths afar,
    With flowers more bright and rare,
But what of them, unless that Hand
    Have cast its Shadow there ?

Not fortune's brightest beams I ask
    About my path to play,
If Duty with its guiding hand
    But point my onward way !

THE POET.

DECK thyself in splendour, Earth!
Thy most gorgeous hues display!
Hill and dale,
Mountain and vale,
All in green
Of spring-time seen,
Celebrate the glorious day
Of the Poet's birth!

All around
Sweet music sound
Soul-entrancing harmony!
Mingle in tone
The sea's soft moan
With the faint and tender sigh
Of winds that play
On its bosom all day,
Till stars arise
In evening skies,
Then, awed by the stillness, die away.

Birds, your sweetest songs awake!
Into strains of rapture break
For the Poet's sake
On his day of birth!
Borne his soul on seraph wings,
Messages from Heaven he brings
To the sons of earth!

Poet, with thy dreamy eyes,
Deeply blue like southern skies!
Golden curls, in clusters bright,
On thy brow a crown of light!
Parted lips, that seem to sigh
With some inward melody,
That from out thy heart's profound
Seeks to vent itself in sound,—
Exile of a lovelier sphere,
Come! reveal its wonders here!

See him in his radiant youth
With sublime ambition fired,—
Holy confidence inspired,
Girt in armour of God's truth!

Of spirit meek yet bold,
And resolute to uphold
Freedom's fair cause against a world of foes—
In his own might

He stood to fight
For the clear truth thro' false and hollow shows;
The worship of his heart like incense rose
Morning and noon and night—
His life was one long hymn of praise—
And wheresoe'er
He turned his gaze
On forms of earth and sea and air,
The light divine
Still seemed to shine
Upon him everywhere.

He saw God in the sun,— the sea,—
On mountain heights, in valleys low,—
In all the simplest things that be,
From stars that glow
With feeble ray,
To flowers that blow
But one short day.
Thro' the whole earth he seemed to trace
In all its majesty and grace
Th' expression of his Maker's face !

Love filled his soul to overflow :—
He lifted up his voice in song,—
Now sweet and low,
Now deep and strong,
His melodies were borne along

Into all lands,
Reaching remotest strands,
Echoing the wildest, loneliest haunts among.

Now with tender melting strain
He soothed the suff'rer's pain ; —
The heart love-lorn
With anguish torn
He won to hope again.
And now with voice of thunder he awoke
The slumb'ring souls of men,
The hermit in his lonely cave,
The captive in his living grave,
The million poor, that groan
Beneath the despot's yoke,
The monarch on his throne,
Tyrant alike and slave,
All, awe-struck, heard the mighty tone
Of this inspirèd One.

As all true poets sing, he sung,
Of liberty — the cause divine —
And fearless taught God's truth.
He pleaded for the laws benign
Of peace and love and ruth.
Men said : " He hath an Angel's tongue,
'Tis wonderful to hear !"
And crowding round from far and near

With loud acclaim his praises rung,
And poured their flatt'ries in his ear.

Of rich, and poor, and high, and low,
The idol he became.
Young hearts would glow,
And tears would flow
At mention of his name.
He reached the loftiest pinnacle of fame —
A giddy height,
Where few, too few, alas! have stood upright!

The world's applause like poison stole
Sure working thro' his inmost soul.
By slow degrees he felt arise
A mist between him and the skies;
And in the mist he seemed to trace
In vivid likeness his own face;
And wheresoe'er
He turned his gaze
On forms of earth, and sea, and air,
The mist still seemed to settle there.

He saw no more God's image — but his own.
The rainbow
And the sunset's glow —
The grass and flowers

And fragrant showers,—
Hill, lake, and wood,
Fountain and flood,
All things, tho' beautiful and good,
Could teach him nothing now.
God spoke to him no more :
He heard alone
His own voice in the water's roar,
And in the wind's low moan.
Vain-glory, worldly fame
The idols of his heart became,—
And in his mind
(To nature's influence cold and dead)
With petty cares and thoughts enshrined
His own vain self he worshipped in God's stead.

Above, below, on whatsoe'er
He gazed of earth, and sea, and air,
The mist would rise
Before his eyes
And show his own face everywhere.

His once sweet voice discordant grew,—
He sung no more the beautiful and true,—
But poured out a wild strain
Of discontents and yearnings vain,
The morbid workings of a brain,
That colours all things in its own dark hue.

How is he fall'n from his height,
The once aspirant son of light!
His joyless strains delight no more
The crowds, that thronged his path before;
He is passed out of sight
And memory of men—
Nor ever will he sing again
The songs, that charm'd the world of yore!

O, Poet! in this dark and perilous clime.
This world of death and time—
With snares beset, without, within,
Wouldst thou the crown of fame immortal win,
Close up thine ears to aught of praise or blame,
Which men may heap upon thy name!
Say, fearless, that thou hast to say!
And turning not to left or right,
But keeping God in sight—
Go calmly on thy way.
So, a true poet, prophet, shalt thou be—
Nor mist shall rise
To cheat thine eyes—
And hide the Sun—thy God—from thee!

DOMENIC.

" LIGHTS of the world," far shining, where are they ?
Who are they, set on hallowed eminence
To beacon souls, that thro' this night of life
Are yearning towards the dawn ? that, in the midst
Of this confused, distractive whirl and war
Of good and ill,—these soul-obstructing clouds
That dim our being,—shine like stars of hope
Serene, eternal o'er tempestuous time ?
Oh rare and lonely prophets of the truth,—
(Like Him, the Great Anointed) that arise
In lowliest corners of the earth, to make
Faint sign in life, but, dying, leave behind
A blaze of light all ages to illume,—
Bear witness, how, by men cast out and scorned,
Your martyr spirits wander lone,—unloved—
Sent out from God's own ark, like the poor dove,
When on the briny waste she sought in vain
Some spot of green to rest her wearied wing!

For men are wedded to their idols still:
Still fond, beneath some weak disguise to veil
The awful eyes of truth, that pierce the soul
And lay its inmosts bare,—would rather grope
In darkness among shadows, than step forth
Faithful and brave into the open day,
Casting aside those shackles tyrannous
Of custom, circumstance, opinion, wrought,
And in the sight of angels ministrant
Steer straight and strong their God-directed course.
" How long, O Lord, how long ?"—when he, the last,
The youngest of the chosen band, stood forth,
Girt with an hundred graces, to unfold
His hallowed mission,—ah! what sound arose
Of hope and exultation, that in him
Had dawned an era of new life on earth,
The long-expected reign of charity!
—A fair and saintly soul had Domenic.
Aspiring and inspired: at times perchance
All overful of human tenderness,
And even to weakness pitiful: still prone
To *pray for* sinners, rather than upbraid.
Most bountiful of nature,—fain to hold
All being in that world of love, his heart,
And still have love to spare. A joyous light
Was wont to play around his brow in youth,
Which paled and faded, when,—his soul oppressed
By sense of his high dawning destiny,—

He. like his master, sought in solitude
New revelation and new strength from heaven.
He pondered pitiful the troublous state
Of this poor world,—so fair to outward sight,
God-gifted with all nature's loveliness,
Fit habitation for an angel race :—
He pondered, heart-sore, man's ingratitude,
Whose reckless passions change to very hell
This seeming paradise. From haunts deep hid
Of crime and wretchedness, thro' every range
Of orders and societies of men,
His mind explored, for some redeeming sign,
Some germ of better life,—but all in vain ;
The same sad picture rose on every side.—
The powerful few oppress,—the million poor,
Enslaved by ignorance, from time to time
Goaded to madness, earthquake-like, break forth
To wreak on tyrants quick and dire revenge !
Ah ! where religion's reconciling sway,
All wrongs adjusting, healing mutual wounds,
Forbearing. bearing ever ! grown a *name*—
An empty sound, which but as prelude serves
For harsher discords, vindicating oft
Earth's foulest passions with a show of heaven.
Like "whited sepulchres on dead men's bones !"
O world, nigh hopelessly to ill resigned,
Wherein such monstrous and distorted fruit
Can grow—from parent tree so wondrous fair

K

By springs divine in God's own Eden reared!
Sore sighed dejected Domenic, yet spake
In resolute mild tone : " I will go forth
Strong in thy patience and thy love, dear Lord,
And preach once more thy law of peace to men!
Upon the tombs of thy rejected saints,—
By all the toils and sorrows consecrate
Of prophet and apostle — by thine own
Long-suffering life, thy death compassionate,
Thyself divine — I will invoke, adjure
Their stubborn hearts to melt, their hands to join,
And prayers ascend in Christian brotherhood!"
When first the voice of Domenic arose
Deep-toned and clear, and startling among men
(As 'twere from other worlds a sudden sound
Of warning — mournful, merciful,) a thrill
Of awful rapture struck from heart to heart,—
Crowds gathered round, all earnestness to catch
The faintest murmur of his eloquent lips,
To note each fitful change from mild to stern,
Alternate light and shade o'er lineaments,
That angels might have loved to gaze upon!
They clasped their hands, and prayed and sobbed by
            . turns,
And deemed all goodness possible — and cried,
" A prophet has arisen!"   But Domenic
Well knew, that he who is to-day "a God"
To-morrow is a "murderer" among men,

And heard their praises as the sound of winds,
Whose soothing sighs at dawn may haply change
To howlings ere the night.   He to his task
Devoutly turned,—deaf to the luring voice
Of ease and pleasure,—blind to all fair sights,
That pressed upon his path.—dead even to dreams
Of innocent endearments,—lawful joys,
And peaceful home delights :—he, strong and true
To his divine behest, in youth's full prime
Took up his cross, and left the world behind !
Early and late, wherever sick or sad,
Or poor or guilty, needed help and prayer,
Counsel and consolation, there was he—
A faithful witness in his daily life,
That priests are ministers, not masters, sent
By Him, their Lord, who washed His servants' feet.
But evermore each day it wrung his heart
To mark, how man from man would stand aloof,
Nor join in social joys and gen'rous acts,
Nor worship side by side their common Lord
For sake of some distinction frail and nice,
Some trifling difference in form or creed.
Oh ! cursed conceit, which makes each man conceive
Himself the special care and pride of Heav'n !
More curs'd still the fruit, such temper bears
In shameful strifes and discords blasphemous !
With pious ardour, aye from shrine to shrine
Went Domenic ;—wherever knee was bowed

For sake of Christ,— wherever mass was sung
Or prayer upraised,— beneath cathedral dome,
In way-side chapel and conventicle,
In most despisèd haunt, where two or three
Were gathered in the name of Him he loved,
With sympathy all worshippers among
He knelt, and prayed, and pleaded still for peace
And brotherly communion;—firm in trust
To form at last an Universal Church
In " unity of spirit," not of creed,
In " bonds of peace and righteousness of life."
Vague hope, poor Domenic! On every side
Now rose the rulers and the priests of men
In murmurings against him, " Who is this ? "
They cry :—" Bold innovator, that would turn
All hearts against us ? lawless breaking down
The ancient barriers between creed and creed ?
Presumptuous, that would cool our holy ire
Against the foes of Heaven! that speaks of peace
Where peace is not, nor can be!—dares upbraid
The rich with arrogance and selfishness,
And plead the poor man's cause! if he prevail,
All pomp, all privilege for us, is lost—
Dominion, glory, hopelessly o'erthrown!"—
What fate had Domenic such foes among ?
With withering accusation, taunt and scoff,
They strove to blight his fame: thereby to break
His gentle spirit :—but as one, who sees

And hears, yet heeds not, he his course pursued
Unshrinking, unreviling,— nor betrayed,
Save by the deep'ning pallor of his cheek,
The waning lustre of his resolute eye,
How sharp the serpent stung.   Dismayed, enraged
To find his fortitude resist their spleen,
With cries of " heretic" and " infidel,"
They stript him of his priestly robe, (that robe,
Which he became so well!) and drove him forth
With scorn and curses to the wilderness.
Forlorn, heart-broken, wandered Domenic,—
His fruitless labours ended,— all his hopes
Of man's regeneration crushed and dead.
Thro' bleak unkindly solitudes, afar
From sound or sight of living thing,— on, on,
Towards desolation and despair, he went,
Till dawned in view the wild sea-shore, and fell
Upon his ear its murmur, like the tones
Of some familiar friend, who still is true
When all else fails us :— wasted, wan, and weak
With toil and anguish, like a wearied ghost
That seeks its sepulchre, he grateful sunk
Upon the soft cool sand, and closed his eyes.
As courting sleep or death : the gentle sea
With plaintive moanings soothed his soul and sense.
When lo! all sudden startling, on the air
Broke forth a sigh of such distressful sound,
As might have waked an answer from the stones!

Slow on his side turned Domenic, and saw,
Or deemed he saw, with mazèd dreamful eyes,
A maiden, wondrous beautiful and strange,
Who sat upon a rock in woeful plight,
With claspèd hands and wand'ring yellow hair;
And looks exceeding sorrowful and sweet.
" Be comforted," she said, " thou noble heart!
Last, bravest champion of a cause sublime!
The memory of thy martyrdom shall live
Sure working among men! The seed once sown,
Still hope we for the harvest! Look on me;
For whom so well and wisely thou hast striven!
The angel of the Catholic Church am I,
Who watched on Calvary the awful hour,
When earth was rent, and graves disclosed their dead —
Who sat beside the sepulchre, and stood
Among the twelve on day of Pentecost!
Since when, ah me! o'er all the earth in vain
I seek for sanctuary; — on every side
The sounds of strife and tumult greet mine ear:
Each man is set against his neighbour. — Where
The blest communion? where the Christian Church,
Whose all-embracing heart is charity?
Ah, happy thou! whose sun, already set,
Shall rise on worlds divine, whilst I am doomed
An outcast here till my appointed day,
When love and peace victorious must resume
O'er man their lost supremacy!" No more

Her voice, aye fainter grown, heard Domenic!
The calm, cold sleep of death had wrapt his limbs :
Now rose the moon, and, veiled beneath its beams,
All pale and grand he lay,—until the sea
(Like some fond mother yearning o'er her child)
With low funereal murmurs tenderly
Lifted the corpse, and gave it burial due
Among the gorgeous trophies of the deep.

TO CECILE.

GRACE, peace, and love, crown all thy life with light!
Bless thee, as with thy lovely presence thou dost bless
All hearts around thee!   Give thee full content
Of all, thou deem'st most dear and beautiful!
And, if some choicest gift, precious past price,
The bountiful angels hold in store for one
They worthiest deem, such gift of gifts be thine!
Then shalt thou be as blithe as thou art good,
Meek, wise, and tender; and the grace of youth,
That clings to thee like love, shall never fade,
But year by year thy spiritual being show
More radiant, as its outward garb grows dim!
A blessing on thy fair and innocent face!
And on thy sunny hair, and the mild light
Of thy kind eyes; and oh, if wish, or hope,
Or prayer of love avails, thou shalt be blest!

C. F. B. M.

London :—STRANGEWAYS & WALDEN (late G. Barclay), Printers,
28 Castle Street, Leicester Square.